Addie McCormick

AND THE MYSTERY OF THE SCRAPBOOK

Leanne Lucas

D1517794

HARVEST HOUSE PUBLISHERS
Eugene, Oregon 97402

Addie McCormick and the Mystery of the Missing Scrapbook

Copyright © 1992 by Leanne Lucas
Published by Harvest House Publishers
Eugene, Oregon 97402

Library of Congress Cataloging-in-Publication Data

Lucas, Leanne, 1955–
    Addie McCormick and the mystery of the missing scrap-
book / Leanne Lucas.
        p.   cm. — (Addie adventure series ; bk. 2)
    Summary: Addie and Nick need God's help in under-
standing racial intolerances as they witness the prejudice of
some of their classmates toward a Mexican American boy
and pursue the secret of a stolen scrapbook belonging to
their adult Japanese American friend Amy.
    ISBN 1-56507-063-1
    [1. Racism—Fiction.   2. Prejudices—Fiction.
3. Mexican Americans—Fiction.   4. Japanese
Americans—Fiction.   5. Christian life—Fiction.
6. Mystery and detective stories.]   I. Title.   II. Series:
Lucas, Leanne, 1955–   Addie adventure series ; bk.
2.
PZ7.L96963Ad   1992
[Fic]—dc20   92-10569
                                                      CIP
                                                      AC

Printed in the United States of America.

CHAPTER 1

Rice Balls
and Scrapbooks

"I'm not eating those." Nick wrinkled his nose at the bowl of sticky white things on the table. "What are they, anyway?"

"They're called rice balls," Addie replied. "My mom has had them before. She says they're good." Addie couldn't quite believe that herself, and Nick heard the hesitancy in her voice.

"You can eat them, then. I'm not."

"Just try one," Addie said. "It won't kill you to be polite. It was nice of Amy to invite us for tea. I think that's kind of special to the Japanese."

"Tea makes my stomach hurt," Nick grumbled.

There were footsteps in the hall outside the room and Addie lowered her voice. "Please, Nick," she whispered, "don't embarrass me."

"You'll be a whole lot more embarrassed if I throw up in the rice balls," he whispered back.

Amy hurried into the room and almost ran into the two children standing by the door. "Oh, excuse me," she said. "Thank you for waiting. I wanted to put away my garden tools before we had tea."

She slipped out of a pair of funny-looking wooden shoes and left them on the mat by the door. "Please." She motioned to the children to do the same. Addie stepped out of her flip-flops and Nick supressed a sigh as he bent down to untie his hightops.

"Come in, come in," she insisted when they remained standing by the door in their barefeet. Addie crossed the hardwood floor and knelt beside the long, low table where Amy was pouring green tea into delicate lacquered tea cups. Nick dropped awkwardly to his knees beside her. They looked expectantly at Amy and she smiled.

"You may relax," she whispered.

Addie realized she'd been holding her breath. She giggled and sat down with her legs crossed, Indian-style. Nick muttered something and tried to cross his legs too. His knees stuck out at odd angles and he bumped the table, spilling his tea.

"Be careful," Addie admonished him.

Nick frowned. "Well, what am I supposed to do with my legs?"

"You may sit however is most comfortable for you, Nick." Amy set the matching teapot on a hot plate on the table and gracefully sank to the floor, tucking her legs to one side.

"I thought this was a sacred ceremony with rules and everything," Nick said. "I don't want to do anything wrong."

"Oh, this is not the *Cha-no-yu*, the traditional Japanese tea ceremony," Amy laughed. "Even I have not attended one of those for many years. Too much work! I just wanted to spend some time with my new friends. Please, do whatever is necessary to make yourself comfortable."

"Got a chair?" Nick muttered and Addie jabbed him with her elbow.

Amy picked up the bowl of rice balls and offered them to the children. Addie took one and cast a warning glance at Nick. He ignored her look but took a rice ball and bit off a small piece on the end. His eyes lit up.

"Say, this is pretty good." He took another, larger bite. "What are those little black things in the rice?" he asked with his mouth full.

Amy smiled and winked at Addie. "Fish eggs."

Some of the enthusiasm left Nick's face, but he continued chewing.

"What's the black stuff on the outside?" Addie asked before she tasted it.

Amy's smile deepened. "Seaweed."

Nick looked frantically for a place to spit out what was left in his mouth. Addie laughed and poked him in the side.

"Go ahead and swallow it, Nick. You thought it was good until you knew what it was."

Nick closed his eyes and swallowed. "There. Your turn."

Addie took a deep breath and bit into her rice ball. To her surprise, it really did taste very good.

Nick watched her and decided to finish his own. "I just won't look at it," he said.

Next, Addie picked up her small tea cup with both hands and sipped cautiously. The tea was scalding hot, and bitter.

Nick took a quick slurp and then spit most of his back into the cup. "It's hot!" he gasped.

"Of course it's hot," Addie frowned. "Couldn't you see it steaming?" She glared at her friend and he glared back. Afternoon tea was not Nick's idea of a good time.

Amy only smiled. "Perhaps I could show you some of my family's art collection while the tea cools."

"That'd be great!" Nick jumped to his feet and bumped the table once more, this time spilling everyone's tea. "Uh, sorry."

"Clod," Addie whispered as she stood up and Nick blushed.

"I said I was sorry," he mumbled.

"It's all right, Nick. We'll clean it up in a minute." Amy's serene voice reassured the boy and he made a face at Addie.

"As you can see, I do not have everything un- packed yet." Amy gestured to boxes that sat on the floor along the walls. "I have much to do before I can call this room my home."

Addie knelt beside an open box and gently lifted a porcelain vase out of its paper wrappings. "This is beautiful," she breathed and traced her finger over green vines that trailed through a sea of tiny blue fish.

"My vase collection has been in the family for many years," Amy said. "That one belonged to my great-grandmother's great-grandmother."

Addie did some quick mental math and carefully put the vase back in the box. "That's almost 200 years old!"

Amy nodded. "My family has always placed great value in art."

"These are cool," Nick said as he squatted down to get a closer look at several pine *bonsai* trees.

"Cool?" Amy laughed softly. "I suppose that is a compliment. My father taught me the art of bonsai. He was a master at it. Those belonged to him before he died."

"Is it hard to do?" Nick asked.

Amy nodded. "It takes many years and much patience to learn."

One wall was filled with paper scroll paintings. "I hung these first to get them off the floor," Amy explained, "but I will rearrange them when everything else is unpacked."

"Are any of them 200 years old?" Nick asked.

"No," Amy said. "This is the oldest." She pointed to an elegantly simple painting of a bird in flight. "It belonged to my grandfather. I will hang it in the *tokonoma*."

"In the toko-what?" Nick stumbled over the strange word.

"Tokonoma," Addie repeated for him.

Nick raised his eyebrows. "So what's a tokonoma, Miss know-it-all?"

It was Addie's turn to blush and shrug, so Amy answered for her. "A traditional Japanese home has a special corner decorated with flowers and a painting. It is called a tokonoma and it shows our reverence for the beauty in nature. I have moved many times and I find I never feel quite at home until I have the tokonoma decorated."

Addie stopped in front of a group of three paintings. The subject matter in each was the same—three young girls—but the size of the scroll and the age of the girls progressed together. The smallest showed three toddlers playing amidst a spattering of brightly colored flowers. The next was larger and showed three school-aged girls engrossed in the plight of a fallen bird. In the largest, and the last, three young women sat sedately on a bench.

"These paintings are so detailed you can tell they're the same girls," Addie said. "You can even tell who's who from the first painting to the last."

"Show me," Amy ordered, and Addie pointed in succession to each girl as she changed from painting to painting.

"Exactly right," Amy smiled.

Nick pointed to the oldest girl in the last picture and said, "She looks like you, Amy."

Amy's smile faded. When she said nothing, Nick tried again.

"I guess they all kind of look like you." That didn't sound right either.

"Not that you all look alike—I mean—" He looked to Addie for help, but her eyes were closed and she was shaking her head.

"What's this?" he asked desperately, picking up a large scrapbook that sat on the table with the tea. He flipped the book open and Addie caught a quick glimpse of some pencil sketches before Amy took it swiftly from his hands.

"That is quite personal," she replied softly and slipped it into the top drawer of a desk. She pushed something under the drawer and there was a soft click.

Addie knelt by the table once again and sipped her drink. "Now the tea's cold," she joked, but no one smiled.

"Perhaps we can try this another day, once I am settled and my things are in order," Amy said.

"Sounds good to me." Nick hurried to the door and grabbed his shoes. "Thanks, Amy. See you later."

Addie stood up, anxious to follow him. She paused in front of Amy and tried to smile.

"Thanks for the . . . the . . . thanks," she finished in confusion. She slipped back into her flip-flops and ran down the hall to catch up with Nick.

CHAPTER 2

Unexpected Friends

"What went wrong?" Nick whispered as they hurried down the back steps into the late August sunshine.

"I'm not sure," Addie answered. "But..."

"It wasn't my fault!" Nick burst out before Addie could accuse him. "How was I to know she'd be so sensitive about those paintings?"

"You couldn't know," Addie agreed. "But..."

"And that scrapbook was laying out there with everything else." Nick interrupted again. "If she didn't want us to see it, she should have put it away to begin with."

"I know," Addie nodded, "but you—don't interrupt me," she warned when Nick started to sputter once more. She picked up her bike and started down the driveway. Nick was close behind her on his 10-speed. "You didn't have to say all Japanese look alike!"

"That's not what I said!" Nick protested.

"That's what it sounded like."

"Yeah, it did, didn't it?" Nick's face was glum and he pedaled in silence.

"Still," Addie mused, "that doesn't explain why she wouldn't talk about the paintings or show you her scrapbook. It almost seemed as if she had something to hide."

Nick gave a loud hoot. "Don't get started, Addie! One mystery this summer was enough, don't you think?"

Addie grinned. It had only been a month since she and Nick had discovered the secret past of their elderly neighbor, Eunice Tisdale. "Miss T.", as they called her, had lived a very interesting life 45 years earlier and because of it, had recently come into a rather large sum of money. That money was being used to remodel her 100-year-old mansion, and pay the wages of a live-in companion, namely Amiko Takahashi.

"Miss T. asked us to make Amy feel welcome. She'll have a fit if she finds out what happened," Addie said.

"Why don't you pray she doesn't find out?" Nick teased, and Addie stuck her tongue out at him. Nick took any opportunity he had to rib her about praying. But Addie knew deep down he respected the power of prayer, so she was good-natured about his teasing.

"I bet Amy won't say anything about it," he decided. "I don't think she was mad. If anything, she seemed scared. Maybe you're right."

An approaching car tooted its horn and both children waved as it passed. Miss T. waved back and continued down the road to her home.

"I still can't believe she's driving a car," Nick said.

"She's doing a lot of things she's never done before," Addie answered. When they first met Miss T., she had been quite deaf. With the extra money came hearing aids and the courage to try for a driver's license. To everyone's surprise (Miss T.'s included), she passed the test. The next day she came home in a new Buick Oldsmobile.

"She drives like an old lady." Nick couldn't help but sound a little disgusted.

"She *is* an old lady, Nick," Addie said. "I'd be worried if she drove like a 30-year old."

"I guess so," Nick agreed. "Say, what time is it?"

Addie glanced at her watch. "About 3 o'clock. I've only got an hour before I have to be home. Then we're going to town to eat supper and buy my school clothes."

"School." Gloom filled Nick's voice. "I'm trying not to think about it."

"Why?" Addie asked. "I can't wait. I love school."

"Oh, I don't mind school, it's just..." Nick hesitated, then changed the subject. "Let's go to the creek, okay?"

"Sure." Addie loved the creek they often waded in. It was actually a drainage ditch for the corn and bean fields that surrounded their houses. It had been there for many years, long enough to have trees and wild flowers growing down its banks. The creek itself was fairly shallow and there were always schools of minnows darting along its rocky bottom.

They parked their bikes behind some bushes just off the road and slid down the bank to the water below. Addie slipped out of her flip-flops and waded in. Nick stopped to untie his sneakers, and Addie splashed water at him.

"Cut it out," he grouched.

"What's the matter, Nick? Are you really worried about starting school?"

Nick shrugged. "I guess. I've never been to a new school before."

Addie nodded. "It is kind of scary starting all over again. When my dad was a minister we moved three different times. Then he took the job here, managing the radio station, and he promised we wouldn't move again for a long time. I hope he's right."

Nick waded into the water, stooping to pick out several smooth, flat rocks from the creek bed. He tossed them downstream and watched as the first one skimmed the top of the water three times.

Addie continued. "It takes a while, but you make friends. I always do."

"You've got a head start," Nick answered. "You already know lots of kids from your church. I don't know anybody."

Addie tried to ignore the twinge of hurt feelings in the pit of her stomach. "What am I, chopped liver?" she joked.

"You know what I mean," Nick growled.

Now Addie was puzzled. "No, I don't."

"I don't want to hang around with a . . . I mean, what will the other guys think if I'm seen with . . .

oh, never mind." Nick hurled the last stone into the water and it plunked to the bottom. The only other sound was the buzz of a small plane flying low overhead.

The twinge in Addie's stomach turned into a knot and she spoke slowly. "I know what you mean."

She waded back to her flip-flops and dried the bottoms of her feet on the grass.

"Come on, Addie, don't get mad," Nick pleaded. "I just don't want to hang around with a girl. The other guys will think I'm a wimp."

"I hadn't planned on carrying your books," Addie snapped. "I just thought I could introduce you to some of the guys from my church."

Nick raised his eyebrows and his expression clearly showed he didn't consider that much of an improvement.

"Oh, yeah, I forgot. Christians are wimps, too, right?" She scrambled up the bank. Nick splashed out of the water, grabbed his shoes and came after her.

"Addie, wait!"

"I've got to get home," she yelled over her shoulder. "We'll be leaving soon."

"You've got to come back to my house for just a minute," Nick called. "You promised your mom you'd bring home the cookie sheets she wanted to borrow, remember?"

Addie paused for a moment and sighed. "That's right. Okay, let's go."

They pedaled in silence. Nick still carried his shoes and the laces flapped noisily against his leg.

When they arrived at his house, Mrs. Brady was peering out the window. She saw the children and came out the back door almost immediately. The screen slammed shut behind her. She balanced Nick's baby sister, Jesse Kate, on one hip and waved a letter in her other hand.

"Can I pick up those . . ." Addie began, but Mrs. Brady didn't hear her.

"Nick, we've got a letter from Brian Dennison and his father!" she exclaimed.

Nick's face lit up. "Are they back in the states?" he asked.

"Mr. Dennison can only stay for a short time," Mrs. Brady answered, "but I think you'll be very interested in what he has to say."

"Who are the Dennisons?" Addie's curiosity was aroused despite her anger. "Where have they been?"

"Brad Dennison is a corporate executive for *Club America*," Mrs. Brady answered. "He sets up franchises of their restaurant in foreign countries. He and Brian have lived in Germany the past two years. Before that, they were in France. Now Mr. Dennison is being sent to Japan to negotiate a franchise there."

"When is he leaving?" Nick asked.

"The end of next week," Mrs. Brady answered.

Nick's expression darkened. "We won't get much of a visit with them, will we?"

Mrs. Brady laughed. "Longer than you think. Brad will be traveling between cities the first three months, so he wants Brian to stay in the states and join him after Christmas."

Nick was off his bike in a flash and grabbed his mother by the shoulders. "He's staying here, isn't he, Mom?"

"Of course, honey! I wouldn't want them to even think of sending him somewhere else. I'm just so glad you're going to have a friend to start school with." Mrs. Brady smiled at her ecstatic son and Jesse Kate squealed and clapped her hands.

"YES!" Nick shouted and ran toward the open garage, leaping to slap both hands against the top of the door. "YES!"

Addie touched Mrs. Brady lightly on the arm. "I'll pick up those cookie sheets tomorrow, if that's okay. My mom doesn't need them until then."

"What? Oh, of course, Addie, that will be fine. See you then." Mrs. Brady turned back to Nick.

Addie picked up her bike and rode slowly down the drive. The knot in her stomach had tightened.

CHAPTER 3

The First Day

Addie sat at the kitchen table and pushed three soggy Cheerios around her cereal bowl with the tip of her spoon. She gave a small sigh, then dropped the spoon with a clank.

"You look very pretty today, honey," her father remarked and reached over to pull the long, black braid that hung down the middle of her back. Then he thought better of it and patted her shoulder instead. "That looks too nice to pull," he smiled. "Did your mom do the braid or did you?"

"Who do you think?" Addie grinned reluctantly, since her impatience with anything like that was a well known fact in the McCormick household.

"Well, it's a very nice way to start off the new school year," he said. "Are you ready for your first day at Heritage?"

"Sure." Addie didn't elaborate and her father frowned.

"Come on, honey, what is it? You've been moping around here all weekend. Mom and I have both noticed. I know it's difficult starting another new school, but you seem to be taking this harder than you did last time."

Addie shrugged. "Just first day jitters, I guess. I'll be okay once I get there. I know a few of the kids from church and Nick will be there. With Brian." Addie had told her parents about Brian's arrival the night they went shopping.

Her father sighed. "It's Brian, isn't it?"

Addie nodded and swallowed hard. "I haven't even met him yet, Dad! Everytime I stopped by the Bradys', he and Nick were gone. When I called, Nick kept making excuses about being too busy to come over. Nick won't have anything to do with me now that Brian's here."

"That's not true, Addie. There is a lot to do when you're enrolling in a new school. You know that; you've had to go through it enough times. And it must be twice as hectic when you only have a week to do it."

John McCormick stood up and pulled his troubled daughter to her feet. He embraced her tightly and kissed the top of her head. "I'm sure Nick will introduce you to Brian today and things will work out fine. Just remember, honey, Brian's the one who's going to have the hardest time at this new school. He only has one friend, Nick, and he probably misses his father already. If there's a problem between you and Nick, work it out. But don't make Brian suffer, okay? He's going to need all the support he can get for the next couple of months."

Addie nodded and pillowed her head on her father's shoulder as he said a brief prayer for Addie,

Nick, Brian and the new school year. When he finished, she gave him a bear hug around the neck. "Thanks, Dad."

"You're welcome, kiddo. Ready to go? Get your school supplies while I start the car."

It was a 20-minute drive to the big brick building that served as the consolidated grade school for three small communities in the area. Beginning this afternoon, Addie would ride the bus, but Mr. and Mrs. McCormick always drove her to school the first day of a new year. It was a tradition that gave Addie a feeling of security when everything else around her was changing.

Mr. McCormick walked Addie inside. After exchanging a few words with the secretary, they were admitted to the principal's office. Mr. Stayton's desk was cluttered with papers, but he found Addie's file with little problem.

"Your grades certainly speak well for you, young lady," he said with a smile. "It will be a real pleasure having you here at Heritage."

"Thanks," Addie said.

"Thank you for coming in, Mr. McCormick." The two men shook hands, then Addie's father put one arm around her shoulders and hugged her gently. "We think she's a wonderful girl. I'm sure you'll agree with us once you get to know her." He gave his daughter a quick grin (and a gentle tug on the braid) and left.

"Addie, you'll be in Mrs. Himmel's class this year. I know you'll like her." He paused and looked at the door as if he expected someone. "I'll show you to your class myself, but I was hoping we could wait a few minutes. You're not the only new student in the sixth grade this year. We have five all together. I've already taken two of the others to their classroom, but there are still two boys to arrive. Let's see..." He pushed his glasses down on his nose and rifled through the files on his desk. "Here they are. Nicholas Brady and Brad... no that's his father... Brian, yes, Brian..."

Before Mr. Stayton could finish his sentence, the door to the office opened. Mrs. Brady walked in the room, followed by Nick and Brian Dennison.

"Mrs. Brady, come right in," Mr. Stayton said. "And here we have Nick and Brian as well. Welcome to Heritage, boys."

"Thanks," Brian replied and shook hands briefly with the principal. He was tall, almost half a head taller than Nick, and thin. He had dark brown eyes and straight, dish-water blond hair. He seemed unusually graceful for a boy his size, and carried himself with ease. Addie stared at him, and he returned her stare with an unblinking, friendly gaze.

"Yeah, thanks." Nick stuck his hand out too.

"Class is almost ready to start, so let me get a few more papers you'll need. Oh, excuse me, Addie." Mr. Stayton seemed surprised to find Addie still standing quietly behind him. He made quick introductions.

"Boys, this is Addie McCormick. She's the other new student in your class."

Nick stuck out his hand once more and said solemnly, "How do you do, Addie? It's a pleasure to meet you."

Addie tried to keep a straight face as they shook hands, but it was too much, and they both broke into nervous laughter. Brian grinned broadly and Mrs. Brady shook her head with amusement.

"These two know each other quite well, Mr. Stayton. Addie is our closest neighbor," she explained. "But Addie and Brian have never met."

"Hi," Addie said between giggles.

"Hi," Brian answered, still grinning.

Mr. Stayton smiled with them and thanked Mrs. Brady for bringing the boys. "Let's go now, kids. School has already started. I'll show you to your room."

Several students still lingered in the halls, but moved to their classrooms quickly when they saw Mr. Stayton coming. The noise of a locker slamming and a door opening were the only sounds the children heard as they walked down a long hall and up one flight of stairs.

They were quiet as they made the short trip to their new classroom. Nick kept making faces at Addie when he thought Mr. Stayton wasn't looking, but Addie ignored him for fear she would burst into laughter again. Nick finally gave up his attempts to get her attention when Mr. Stayton stopped in front of a door marked MRS. HIMMEL— Sixth Grade. He opened the door and stepped into the room, motioning Addie, Nick, and Brian to follow him.

"Here are your new pupils, Mrs. Himmel," Mr. Stayton said. "Class, this is Addie McCormick, Nick Brady, and Brian Dennison. Please make them feel welcome."

He handed Mrs. Himmel the folders marked with each child's name and turned to leave. "Feel free to come see me if you have any questions," he told the children before leaving.

Mrs. Himmel glanced briefly at Addie's folder and motioned her to a chair near the windows. "I've looked over most of your records already, Addie. Have a seat next to Hillary. She told me this morning you attend her church. I thought you might like to sit near someone you know."

Addie smiled gratefully at the slender, grey-haired woman and slipped into the seat next to Hillary Jackson, one of the girls in her church youth group.

"Nick?" Mrs. Himmel looked questioningly at the two boys and Nick raised his hand slightly. "Nick, there are two seats near the back. Why don't you and Brian sit there? I believe I have your records as well."

"But Brian," she paused to glance through the folder marked DENNISON, "I don't have much information on you yet. I might need to talk with you after school today if that's . . . oh!"

Her delighted exclamation took everyone by surprise and the room was quiet as Mrs. Himmel began speaking in French.

"Brian, tes dossiers indiquent que tu parles francais couramment" ("Brian, your records say you speak French fluently"), she said.

"Oui, Madame, je suis né à Paris et j'y habitais jusqu'a ce que j'avais peufans" ("Yes, ma'am, I was born in Paris and lived there until I was nine years old"), Brian replied.

"C'est magnifique! J'ai passé deux ans à Paris quand j'assistais à l'université. Peut-être nous pouvons parler de Paris quelquefois." ("That's wonderful. I spent two years in Paris when I was in college. Perhaps we could compare notes sometime.") Mrs. Himmel smiled at Brian.

"Si vous voulez" ("If you like"), he said.

The silence was thick as Brian turned to find the whole class (Addie included) staring at him in amazement. He simply stared back with the same quiet confidence Addie had noticed earlier in the office. Then he walked to his seat and the room began to buzz.

CHAPTER 4

Mr. Yamada

The yellow school bus bounced crazily over the pot holes that characterized country roads in Mason County. Addie paid no attention to the bouncing, and tried to listen patiently to the endless stream of chatter coming from her seatmate. Mariel Cramer was another friend from church, and really very nice, if only she wouldn't talk so much.

"Wasn't school fun today, Addie? I love the first day of school. There's never much to do and everything's new, being in a different grade and all. And there are so many new kids this year. You, and those two," Mariel nodded toward the back of the bus, where Nick and Brian sat, "and the new girls in Mr. Zimmer's sixth grade class . . ."

Addie nodded and tried to keep her attention on what Mariel was saying. She glanced back at Nick and Brian. They were deep in conversation, and Addie strained to hear them six seats away. When she realized it was impossible, she tuned back in to Mariel and her analysis of the sixth grade at Heritage.

"If it weren't for Hillary, I don't think Brian would have said a word, do you Addie? She just kept asking him questions. I don't think he really wanted to talk to her, but he was too polite to say so. Don't you think he's polite, Addie?" Mariel stopped to breathe and Addie jumped into the conversation.

"I don't know him any better than you do, Mariel. I just met him today, too. Say, isn't this your corner?"

Mariel nodded. "Yep. And we were just getting started. Oh, well. Save me a seat in the morning, okay, Addie?"

"I'll try." Addie smiled, wanting to be friends with Mariel, but not sure how long she could stand non-stop talking. When the bus creaked to a stop by Mariel's house, Addie slipped quietly to the empty seat in front of Nick and Brian.

Nick grinned wickedly. "Say, Addie, don't you think your new friend is swell? I think she's just swell. I wish I could see her every day, don't you, Addie? Maybe you can sit with her at lunch, too. I bet she'd like that. You'd like that, wouldn't you, Addie? I can't think of anything better than to listen to Mariel . . ."

"Cut it out, Nick." Addie interrupted him with a frown. "I don't think anyone ever listens to her. Maybe she figures the more she talks the better chance she'll have of getting someone to pay attention."

Nick nodded solemnly. "You're so sensitive, Addie. I wish I could be more like you."

Addie grabbed the notebook Nick was carrying and hit him over the head with it. "What's got into you today?"

Nick laughed. "Nothing. Sorry. I'm just glad to be out of school. Remember where we're going when we get home?" he asked Brian.

"Where?" Addie's curiosity forced her to ask the question, even though she was disappointed. She had hoped they would go bike riding with her.

"Amy called last night and asked me to bring Brian over for tea." Nick held an imaginary cup in his hand and crooked his little finger. Brian chuckled softly at Nick's imitation.

Addie didn't. Nick had been invited to Miss T.'s without her? Her surprise and disappointment must have shown, because Nick added teasingly, "Oh, yeah, she said to bring you along if you wanted to come."

Even though Addie knew Nick was only having fun with her, she was upset. Was he going to treat her like this all the time, now that Brian was here?

Brian sensed her frustration. "The truth is, Addie, she called you first, but you weren't home."

Addie took a deep breath and gave Brian a small grin. *"Thanks,"* she said silently, and she was sure Brian knew how she felt. His small act of kindness gave her the courage to ask him a question.

"Is French the only language you know, Brian?"

"I learned German while we were in Munich, but I don't speak it as well as French," he answered. "I grew up speaking French and English interchangeably, so it's easy for me. German is a little tougher. I hope to learn Japanese, too. I've got a Japanese-English dictionary, but that's all. My dad's going to send me some language materials as soon as he can." At the mention of his father, Brian's voice grew wistful and he looked away from Addie and out the window.

"You'll like Miss T. and Amy." Addie changed the subject. Then a thought occurred to her. "Why don't you ask Amy to teach you some Japanese? I bet she'd enjoy it."

"We're already two steps ahead of you, Addie." Nick answered for his friend. "Why else do you think I said yes to tea? I had *so* much fun at our last engagement, I just couldn't wait to get back?"

Addie laughed at the memory of Nick's lacking social graces. "Just don't spill everyone's tea again. And try to keep yours in your mouth," she replied.

"What?" Now Brian was curious.

"Never mind." Nick brought an abrupt end to the conversation and shoved Brian out of the seat as the bus groaned to a stop in front of the Brady house. "Get your bike and meet us here in five minutes, okay?"

"Sure," Addie said. "I'll tell you later," she mouthed to Brian and he grinned and nodded.

When she got home, Addie flew through the front door and into the kitchen. "Hi, mom," she said and planted a quick kiss on her mother's cheek. "Can I go to Miss T.'s? Amy invited us for tea."

"Again? I thought you just—oh, that's right, it didn't work out, did it? I suppose so. How was school . . . Addie!" Mrs. McCormick shook her head at the swinging door.

Addie grabbed her bike from the garage and pedaled out the drive. She could see Nick and Brian riding lazy circles in the road and hurried to catch up with them. Soon the three were around the corner and Miss T.'s mansion was in sight.

Two months ago, no one would have called this house a mansion. But the unexpected fortune Miss T. had acquired allowed her to make drastic improvements. With the windows and roof repaired, a new paint job, and beautiful landscaping, the house was once again majestic. Miss T. called it her "painted lady." That was the name given to houses painted in a Victorian style, with the body of the house one color, the trim painted another and accent pieces painted yet another. Miss T. had chosen ivory, dark blue and beige, and the house seemed particularly warm and inviting today. Addie tried to view the place as Brian would, for the very first time. She was impressed all over again, and so was he.

"Whew," he whistled softly. "Is this lady rich?"

"Kind of," Nick answered and he and Addie exchanged glances. Addie felt some comfort in the knowledge that she and Nick shared a secret Brian didn't know. It had been decided from the beginning that they wouldn't tell Brian about Miss T.'s past. Nick had argued that Brian would never tell her secret once he understood how important it was to keep the past private. Now that she had met Brian, Addie agreed with him, but Mr. McCormick had made the final decision so Addie and Nick had taken a vow of silence.

"There she is," Nick said as they pulled into the long driveway that gleamed and sparkled with white rocks. Miss T. was on her knees in a flower bed and looked up at the sound of gravel crunching. She shaded her eyes and struggled awkwardly to her feet.

Nick slid to a stop by Miss T. and she frowned at the black mark he made.

"Sorry," he grinned.

Addie and Brian came to a more sedate stop and Addie made quick introductions.

"Hello, Brian," said Miss T. and stuck out her hand. He shook it and they appraised one another carefully for a second or two before Miss T. smiled. "I'm glad you came. I was getting tired of digging bulbs. I'm too old for this."

"No you're not," Addie said automatically and then grinned at Miss T.'s frustrated grunt.

"Who are you to tell me I'm not old, miss? I ought to make you dig these bulbs. They were your idea, if I remember correctly."

"You're only as old as you think," Addie said brightly.

"Well, I think I'm pretty darn old right now, young lady, so don't you try to tell me any different."

Brian seemed somewhat taken aback at their brisk exchange, but Nick grinned. "You'll get used to her," he whispered.

"Get used to who, Mr. Brady?" Miss T. fixed him with a sharp gaze and Nick winced. Hearing aides had made a world of difference in their conversations with Miss T.

"Where's Amy?" he asked, to change the subject. "She's expecting us."

Miss T. looked surprised. "She is? There's a Mr. Yamada with her right now. I thought he was the company she mentioned this morning."

At that moment, the front door opened and a tiny, very old Japanese man stepped out into the sunshine. His back was to the small group in the driveway, and he appeared not to notice them. Amy came out behind him.

The man spoke, and his voice carried clearly. "Please tell me where they are."

When Amy didn't answer, his voice grew sharp with disapproval. "If you persist in this stubbornness, you will not only harm my family, but your own family name will be disgraced forever."

CHAPTER 5

Unexpected Treasures

Miss T. cleared her throat and Amy and her visitor looked up. The old man frowned at them for a second, then turned back to Amy.

"Please think about what I have said. Goodbye, Amiko-san."

"Goodbye, Oji-san," Amy murmured.

The old man walked stiffly down the front steps and past the children and Miss T. A red car sat at the end of the drive, near the greenhouse, and the driver's door opened. A much younger man jumped out and hurried to help Mr. Yamada. Then they backed down the drive and sped away.

Miss T. broke the silence. "Is everything all right Amy?"

Amy managed a faint smile and n̶ san is concerned for my family," ̶ nation. "I believe his con̶ do not be troubled."

"It must be kinda imp̶ ily is going to be disgra̶ emphasizing the *forever*.

"In Oji-san's generation, honor was one of the Japanese's most important possessions. But what would have been a disgrace 50 years ago does not seem so important today," Amy answered.

"It sure seemed important to him," Nick persisted.

Miss T. spoke up. "Young man, if Amy is satisfied there's no problem, then there's no problem. Drop it." She picked up her spade and marched into the greenhouse.

Nick made a face in her general direction. "Okay, I'll drop it," he muttered.

"Amy, this is Brian Dennison," Addie said. "He's the friend Nick told you about."

Amy's smile was genuine as she greeted Brian. "I am so pleased to meet you. Nick has spoken highly of you and I know he is pleased to have you here. He tells me you are going to join your father in Japan soon."

Brian nodded. "I hope to leave right after Christmas."

"I will pray the time passes quickly for you," Amy said.

Nick rolled his eyes at the mention of prayer, but Brian smiled. "Thanks," he said simply.

Nick gave his friend a surprised look and it was Addie's turn to make a face at Nick. Amy watched silent exchange with some amusement, but said, "Perhaps I can tell you what to expect he Japanese people and teach you some of our

" Brian exclaimed.

"That was easy," Nick said bluntly. "We were hoping you'd get that idea."

"Nick!" Addie whispered, but Amy only laughed.

"It will be a pleasure to tell you about the land of my ancestors," she said.

"Did you ever live in Japan?" Brian asked.

"No," she said. "I was born in America and have lived here all my life. But my parents instilled in us a reverence for many of the Japanese traditions and most of my possessions were inherited from my parents or grandparents. Perhaps you would like to see them?"

"I'd love it," Brian said eagerly, but Nick and Addie hesitated.

Amy saw the look they exchanged and smiled. "Perhaps we could have a cup of tea as well. I am truly sorry we were unable to enjoy our last visit, children."

Nick shrugged and Addie smiled shyly. "That's okay," she answered.

Amy led them through the house and her shoes made a strange clacking noise on the wooden floors. At the door of her room she slipped out of the shoes, and this time Addie saw that the strange wooden thongs were set on platforms. Brian kicked off his sneakers, Addie stepped out of her flip-flops, and Nick sighed loudly as he untied his shoes.

Stepping into Amy's room was like stepping into another world. The stacks of boxes that had cluttered the room only a few days earlier were gone. Woven mats covered the floor and there were several cushions scattered around the room. The long, low table still sat in the center of the room, but that and Amy's desk were her only furniture.

All the paintings had been hung and there were shelves on two walls. One set held the vases Addie had admired. The other set were more like steps that came out from the wall. These held a collection of elaborately dressed dolls.

In one corner the tokonoma had been decorated with the painting of the bird in flight. Underneath the painting, a very tall vase filled with pink and white and yellow gladiolas sat on the floor. Addie walked over to take a deep breath of the fragrant blossoms while Brian began to examine the paintings of the young girls Nick and Addie had seen earlier.

Nick was puzzled. "Where's your bed?" he asked.

Brian spoke up before Amy could answer. "I bet you sleep on a futon, don't you?"

Amy nodded.

"What's a futon?" Nick asked.

"It's bedding you can roll up and put away when you're not using it," Brian answered.

Nick shook his head. "Give me my waterbed any day."

Addie decided to take a closer look at the dolls Amy had displayed. Two of them, a very regal male and female, sat on the top shelf. Beneath them were 12 more dolls, obviously servants. They were all quite fragile looking, with hand-painted faces and exquisite costumes.

"Every girl born into a traditional Japanese family receives a set of dolls at birth," Amy explained.

CHAPTER 5

Unexpected
Treasures

Miss T. cleared her throat and Amy and her visitor looked up. The old man frowned at them for a second, then turned back to Amy.

"Please think about what I have said. Goodbye, Amiko-san."

"Goodbye, Oji-san," Amy murmured.

The old man walked stiffly down the front steps and past the children and Miss T. A red car sat at the end of the drive, near the greenhouse, and the driver's door opened. A much younger man jumped out and hurried to help Mr. Yamada. Then they backed down the drive and sped away.

Miss T. broke the silence. "Is everything all right, Amy?"

Amy managed a faint smile and nodded. "Oji-san is concerned for my family," was her brief explanation. "I believe his concern is unfounded. Please do not be troubled."

"It must be kinda important if everybody's family is going to be disgraced forever," Nick said, emphasizing the *forever*.

"In Oji-san's generation, honor was one of the Japanese's most important possessions. But what would have been a disgrace 50 years ago does not seem so important today," Amy answered.

"It sure seemed important to him," Nick persisted.

Miss T. spoke up. "Young man, if Amy is satisfied there's no problem, then there's no problem. Drop it." She picked up her spade and marched into the greenhouse.

Nick made a face in her general direction. "Okay, I'll drop it," he muttered.

"Amy, this is Brian Dennison," Addie said. "He's the friend Nick told you about."

Amy's smile was genuine as she greeted Brian. "I am so pleased to meet you. Nick has spoken highly of you and I know he is pleased to have you here. He tells me you are going to join your father in Japan soon."

Brian nodded. "I hope to leave right after Christmas."

"I will pray the time passes quickly for you," Amy said.

Nick rolled his eyes at the mention of prayer, but Brian smiled. "Thanks," he said simply.

Nick gave his friend a surprised look and it was Addie's turn to make a face at Nick. Amy watched the silent exchange with some amusement, but only said, "Perhaps I can tell you what to expect from the Japanese people and teach you some of our ways."

"Great!" Brian exclaimed.

"These belonged to my mother, and to her mother before her. New sets were purchased for my younger sisters when they were born. Because I had no daughters to give my dolls to, I have chosen to display them here."

"Most Japanese only display their dolls once a year. They are brought out a few weeks before Girl's Day and packed away as soon as possible after the day has passed."

"Why?" Addie asked.

" Superstitious beliefs," Amy answered. "It is considered bad luck. But since I know there is no such thing, I enjoy my dolls all year round."

She set four small tea cups on the table in the center of the room. "Please have tea with me," she said. "It is already prepared and I would be pleased if you would stay. Oji-san was not interested in tea."

There was an awkward silence, then she hurried on. "It is not too hot to drink today." She smiled at Nick and he turned slightly pink.

The four of them sat down to tea, and Amy served some chocolate chip cookies from the kitchen pantry. "So much for tradition," Nick whispered. They talked comfortably for several minutes, with Amy's gentle questions drawing Brian into the conversation. Soon they learned he was a history buff, his favorite cookies were peanut butter, and he liked to play baseball.

This last bit of information pleased Amy immensely. "You will feel right at home in Japan," she said. "The Japanese are as enamored with baseball as the Americans are with football. In fact, one of the biggest sports events of the year is the *Koko-yakyu*, the high school tournament. It lasts 10 days, and the whole nation watches it on television."

Nick was amazed. "A high school tournament? They must like baseball."

"I hope I get a chance to play on a team," Brian said wistfully.

"No matter where you live, there is always a neighborhood game going on," Amy laughed. "They will welcome your participation, but the competition is fierce," she warned.

"That's okay," Brian replied. "I've played all my life. I'm pretty good." This last remark was simply a statement of fact, made without pride.

Amy smiled at the boy's quiet confidence. "I believe you will do well."

Brian glanced at his watch. "Your mom wanted us home by five, Nick. We'd better get going."

"Please come back soon," Amy told the three of them. "I have enjoyed sharing this time with you. There is much more to tell you if you want to learn all you can about the Japanese people."

"Do you speak Japanese?" Brian's question was an eager one.

Amy smiled. "Oh, yes. I will not try to teach you the language, only some of the expressions and phrases that will be most helpful to you. I am sure your father will be able to arrange for a tutor once you reach Japan."

"This is going to be great," Brian exclaimed once more. "Thanks, Amy."

"It will be a pleasure to help one so eager to learn," she assured him.

The ride home was quiet. Brian watched a small plane circle above them, making its descent to land. "Where's that plane going?" he asked.

"Rankin's Air Field," Addie answered. "It's a private air strip near Miss T.'s house. They have chartered flights to Chicago every day. They give lessons, too."

"You know, there's something I don't understand," Brian remarked as they watched the plane disappear into a corn field. "Why did Amy take a job as a companion for an old lady?"

"Why shouldn't she?" Addie replied. "Miss T. needed help and Amy needed the money."

Brian shook his head. "Amy needs money like I need the flu." Addie and Nick were both surprised at this statement, so Brian explained.

"I'm positive those paintings are originals, and I've seen that artist's name before. Nomura was very famous. Amy has more money hanging on her walls then Miss T. has in her whole house. And that collection of vases? Some of them are almost 200 years old. They're priceless. No, Amy's doesn't need the money. There must be some other reason."

Addie's thoughts jumped unbidden to the scrapbook of sketches hidden in the desk. *Could those be part of the reason?* she wondered, but dismissed the idea quickly. Then she looked at Nick and saw the same question reflected in his eyes.

CHAPTER 6

Unexpected News

Brian dropped onto the bench next to Addie at lunch Tuesday.

"I was right!" he exclaimed. There was no mistaking the excitement in his voice. "Mrs. Hilst helped me look up some information on Japanese art. Those paintings were all done by Yoshio Nomura. He was a very famous Japanese artist. Most of what he painted depicted life in the relocation centers after the bombing of Pearl Harbor."

"Slow down." Nick dropped his plate next to Brian's and threw one leg over the bench next to his friend. "You lost me after the guy's name."

Brian started over. "Yoshio Nomura was a Japanese artist. After the Japanese bombed Pearl Harbor in World War II, he and his family were sent to the relocation center at Manzanar in California. When the war was over, and the Japanese were released, he painted scenes from the camp that became extremely valuable over the next few years. Some of them are in museums here in the states, or in private collections in Japan. There are others that have disappeared."

He paused and looked at Addie and Nick expectantly. Nick's face was blank, but Addie took an educated guess.

"Amy's got them."

Brian grinned. "Of course, Amy's got them! Those are the paintings on her walls! Can you believe it?"

Addie only nodded and Nick took a huge bite out of his slice of pizza.

Brian was dismayed by their lack of interest. "You guys, this is incredible! A find like this only happens once in a lifetime."

"Twice," Nick muttered between bites and Addie giggled.

"What?" Brian asked, but Nick only shook his head and picked up his milk.

"Why do you suppose Amy has them?" Brian continued.

"I don't think it's really much of a mystery." Addie spoke slowly. "The first day Nick and I visited Amy, we were looking at the paintings of the young girls. Nick made the comment that one of the girls in the last picture looked like Amy."

Nick swallowed his last bite of pizza and joined the conversation. "She wasn't happy that I made the comparison, but she didn't deny it, either. Maybe that Nomura guy is her father."

"Oh." Brian's expression changed from excitement to disappointment and back to excitement. "What about Mr. Yamada? Why was he convinced their families were going to be disgraced? Maybe it has something to do with those missing paintings."

"And maybe it's none of our business." Nick's comment took Brian and Addie by surprise, although Addie understood the reasons behind it. Their experience with Miss T. had impressed on both the children the importance of allowing people their privacy. But she couldn't explain this to Brian without going into detail and Brian wasn't going to be put off easily.

"Well, Mrs. Hilst found a book that said those paintings would be incredibly valuable on today's market and . . ."

"Who?" Hillary Jackson sat across from Addie, and had been half-listening to the conversation.

"Mrs. Hilst. The librarian." Brian frowned at the interruption.

"Mrs. Hulsht?" Hillary tried unsuccessfully to imitate the German pronunciation Brian gave to the name. Several other kids at the table laughed as Hillary repeated the word. "Hulsht?"

Brian picked up his fork and jabbed at the pizza on his plate. When he looked at Hillary, his face was blank. "Right. It's a German name. Sometimes I forget to Americanize words when I know their true pronunciation."

"Ooooooo," someone at the end of the table said under their breath, and there were more chuckles.

"Heil Hulsht!" said another in a loud, sharp voice and laughter erupted all around them.

Brian's eyes grew dark. "That's not very funny if you know the history of that expression."

"Of course, students, we must remember our history, mustn't we?" Hillary sat up straight as she spoke and looked down her nose at the others.

Brian picked up his tray and stood up. "See you later, Addie."

Nick was right behind him, but not before giving Addie a venomous look.

What did I do? Addie thought, but she knew the answer. Nick had a tendency to lump all Christians together and she was sure he was going to hold her accountable for Hillary's actions today.

"You really shouldn't tease him, Hillary," she said quietly.

"Can't he take a joke?" The other girl's tone was light but she refused to meet Addie's eyes. "You'd better not hang around with those two, Addie. You're beginning to lose your sense of humor, too." She gave Addie a slight smile but there was a hint of warning in her voice.

Addie stood up. "See you in class," she said.

She dumped her half-eaten pizza in the garbage and carried her apple outside. It was crunchy and tart and a little bit of juice squirted out one side as Addie bit into it. She walked out the back door of the school and through the bus lot to the small park on the other side.

Nick and Brian sat under a large sugar maple tree that was just beginning to change color. Nick looked up and saw her and looked away again. She went on and stood in front of them.

"I'm sorry, Brian," Addie began, but he interrupted her.

"It's okay, " he said. "I'm not mad."

"I thought you were pretty angry when you walked out."

Brian shook his head. "No. But I was getting that way so I thought I'd leave before I said something I would regret."

Nick spoke up. "Your church friends should have left before the conversation even got started."

"It's okay, Nick." Brian punched his friend lightly on the arm and drew circles in the dirt.

"No, it's not," Nick persisted. "I thought Christians were supposed to treat others better than that."

Addie thought so too, so she didn't have an answer. Brian spoke before she had to come up with one. "We're not perfect," he said.

"That's for —" Nick choked back the last word. He stared at Brian and finally managed to stammer, "What do you mean, *we*?"

"You're a Christian." The words slipped out before Addie could stop them.

Brian nodded. He looked Nick straight in the eye. "I tried to tell you a couple of times, but you were never interested. I decided the Lord knew the best time to tell you, so I left it to Him." He paused and grinned. "I guess this was the time."

Addie wanted to turn cartwheels all the way back to the school, but she managed to contain herself. Still, she was almost bubbling over with joy on the inside. She understood now why she thought there was something different about Brian. The quiet confidence that set him apart from the other kids had been Jesus.

Only the look on Nick's face dampened her spirits. The initial shock had given way to resigned acceptance. He sat staring at his friend and shaking his head. Suddenly he turned to Addie with such an accusing frown she took a step backwards.

"What?" she exclaimed. "Don't look at me like that, Nick. I had nothing to do with this!"

"Yeah, right." Nick stood up and dusted off the seat of his pants. Then he pointed a finger at Addie. "Were you praying?"

Addie opened her mouth, then clamped it shut. She darted a quick glance at Brian, who was trying not to laugh. Addie raised her arms in mock dismay.

"Guilty as charged!" Brian shouted and Addie burst out laughing.

"Come on, lunch is over." Nick grumbled, but he grinned reluctantly as Brian waved an imaginary gun at Addie and she walked back to the building with her hands held high.

CHAPTER 7

Angry Words

"Why don't you invite Nick and Brian to church Sunday?" Mr. McCormick was still smiling at the news that Brian Dennison was a Christian.

"When we prayed for Nick I never imagined God would use one of his old friends," Mrs. McCormick remarked.

"Me neither," Addie said. "And I was so worried Brian would be a problem. I guess it just shows you can't second guess God, can you?"

"Mmm, so much wisdom from one so young," her father teased.

Addie ignored him. "You know, I knew there was something different about Brian the first time I met him. He seemed so sure of himself, but he wasn't proud or arrogant. He was just... different."

"The Lord must have done some powerful things in Brian's life," her father commented. "I'd like to think we all make that kind of impression, but I'm not sure we do. I'll be interested in hearing Brian's testimony."

"Now, dear," her mother admonished, "I'm just as excited as you are to hear Addie has another Christian friend. But don't intimidate the boy with 20 questions when you meet him, all right?"

"I'll be a paragon of sensitivity," Mr. McCormick said in a lofty tone.

"A pair of what?" Addie asked.

Her father laughed. "A p-a-r-a-g-o-n. It's only one word. It means a model of excellence or perfection. It's also the name for a perfect diamond over one hundred carats..."

He ended his lecture on the new vocabulary word and waved his hand in front of Addie's face. "Why do your eyes glaze over every time I try to improve your mind, my dear?"

She blinked and giggled. "Sorry, Dad. I was thinking about something else you said, that God must have done something big in Brian's life. Nick told me Brian's mother died while they were living in France. Maybe that's when he came to the Lord. I know he wasn't a Christian the last time Nick saw him. Nick would have told me." She paused. "I wish God would do something like that in my life."

"Addie!"

"Oh, I don't mean I want you to die, Mom."

"Thank you."

"I just wish people would see a difference in me. The kind of difference I see in Brian."

"Well, honey, if your motives are pure and you keep close to the Lord, they will." Her father smiled at her earnest face. "God works differently in everybody's life. He won't use you the way He uses Brian. He'll make you into the person Addie McCormick is supposed to be. Okay?"

"Okay," Addie grinned. "I just wish He'd hurry up!"

"Maybe He should start with patience," her father observed wryly and ducked the wadded-up paper towel Addie threw at him.

Friday morning at school Brian dropped into the chair behind Addie shortly before the bell rang. "Look at this," he exclaimed and plopped a large book on the desk. It was opened to a page of paintings. The most prominent was one of three toddlers in a garden . . . the same picture that hung on Amy's wall.

Addie read the accompanying paragraph out loud. "This painting is the first in a series of three which disappeared from the art world shortly after World War II. The artist, Yoshio Nomura, was famous for his paintings of life at Manzanar, one of several relocation centers opened after Japan bombed Pearl Harbor in 1941. It is generally believed the entire series is part of the private collection of one of Nomura's daughters, who are the subjects of the paintings."

Nick joined them while Addie was reading. He pointed to the oldest girl. "That's Amy."

Brian nodded. "It has to be. But there's something funny about the painting, don't you think? I mean, the way this reads, Nomura painted it at the relocation center. I don't know too much about the center, but I think it was one of the American versions of prisoner-of-war camps."

"America had prisoner-of-war camps?" Addie was shocked.

Brian nodded again. "They weren't as bad as camps in other countries, like Germany, but they weren't the greatest place to be either. And these girls look like they're at a Japanese country club, not a prisoner-of-war camp."

"Mr. Dennison."

Brian, Addie, and Nick all jumped. The rest of the class was quiet, seated and staring. Brian and Nick slipped to their chairs, but not before Mrs. Himmel noticed the large book Brian carried.

"That's pretty substantial reading, Brian. What is the book about?" Mrs. Himmel asked.

"Japanese art," Brian replied. At Mrs. Himmel's surprised expression, Brian continued. "Since I'll be living in Japan, I thought it was important to learn what I could about the Japanese culture."

Hillary Jackson raised her hand. "I think that's a good idea, don't you Mrs. Himmel? Since we live in Illinois, maybe we could study something about Illinois . . . like corn."

Everyone laughed and someone called out, "No, corn-on-the-cob!"

"No, corn bread!"

"No, creamed corn!"

The laughter got louder and Mrs. Himmel pounded on her desk for quiet.

"I think that would be just fascinating," Hillary giggled.

"Quiet," Mrs. Himmel ordered. She gave Hillary a stern look. "Actually, corn would make an interesting unit study. I'm sure you would appreciate some of the more unusual uses we have for corn, Hillary."

Brian tried to hide a smile and Hillary darted a quick glance at him. "Like what?" she asked suspiciously.

"Brian, I think you know what I'm talking about," Mrs. Himmel said.

Brian nodded. "Make-up."

Hillary's artificially red cheeks turned even redder and most of the girls looked uncomfortable. Only the boys snickered this time, and Mrs. Himmel gave Hillary another long look before opening her math book.

"Page seven," she said.

Hillary pulled her book from her backpack and slammed it on her desk. Her pencil dropped to the floor and Addie picked it up. Hillary grabbed it without a thank you and jerked back around in her seat.

Addie glanced at Nick and Brian. Brian shrugged apologetically, but Nick glared, first at Hillary and then at Addie. Addie sighed and opened her math book.

"This is what my dad would call being between a rock and a hard place," she thought.

Math passed quickly, although Hillary's back stayed ramrod straight the entire hour, and she didn't volunteer any answers. Halfway through spelling, Mrs. Himmel called for the morning break, and Hillary left the room without a word.

"Serves her right," Nick muttered in Addie's ear as they filed out the door to the grassy playground.

"I'm sorry, Addie," Brian said. "I hope she doesn't give you a hard time just because she doesn't like me."

"Why doesn't she like you?" Addie mused. "It doesn't make sense. She's been picking on you since the first day of school."

"You don't have to be Einstein to figure that one out," Nick said. "She's jealous."

"Of what?" Addie and Brian chorused.

Nick tapped his forehead with his finger. "Check around, Addie. I bet you'll find out Hillary was top dog in the class until Brain here showed up."

Mariel Cramer had followed them out the door and now she giggled. "Brain. Brian the Brain."

"Oh, no," Nick groaned.

"Mariel, wait," Addie called, but it was too late.

By the end of break "Brian the Brain" had been shortened to "the Brain." There were whispers and laughter when everyone filed back to class . . . whispers that stopped abruptly when Brian entered the room, and then continued for most of the afternoon. Hillary's good mood was restored as well.

Brian ignored the whispers and did his work, but Nick was livid. Mrs. Himmel had to reprimand him twice for not paying attention. And Addie's limited patience snapped when the final bell rang.

"See you Sunday, Addie," Hillary said as they left the classroom. "Why don't you bring 'the Brain' to church with you?" she teased.

"As a matter of fact, I'm going to," Addie snapped, although she hadn't asked Nick or Brian yet.

"That should be interesting," Hillary replied. "I'll be there."

"Why bother?" Addie retorted. "You're obviously not listening to what they're teaching!"

All the color drained from Hillary's face. She turned and stalked from the room.

I don't care, Addie thought as she wiped an angry tear away. *She's been so awful to Brian. I just don't care.*

Just then Brian stuck his head around the corner of the door. "Come on, Addie, you're going to miss the bus." The day's events had not put a dent in his kind smile and Addie was ashamed.

I just wish people would see a difference in me. The kind of difference I see in Brian. Her own words echoed in her ears and brought fresh tears to her eyes.

Some difference, she thought glumly and followed Brian out the door.

CHAPTER 8

Asking Forgiveness

Saturday was cool and clear. It promised to be one of the few absolutely perfect days people in Illinois talked about all the other unpredictable days of the year. But the bright blue sky and soft breeze did little to cheer Addie. She was still disgusted with herself and her temper tantrum of the day before.

Even worse, there was no one to be miserable with. Nick and Brian had gone to town with Nick's family to shop and see a movie. Addie knew Nick was probably still seething over yesterday's events. *Not Brian, though,* she thought. *Nothing seems to get to him. I wonder how he does it? I guess he just walks away, like he did at lunch that day. But he couldn't walk away yesterday. And he still stayed cool. How does he do that?*

The more she thought about it, the angrier she got with herself, so she decided to go for a bike ride. Pedaling down the road, she instinctively headed for Miss. T.'s house. She had never been to Miss T.'s alone, but today seemed like a good time to change that. She stood up to pedal and soon turned into the long drive.

Miss T. was on her knees in the grass in front of the greenhouse. She glanced up at Addie as the young girl came to a stop and dropped her bike on the ground.

"Finally got all the bulbs dug," Miss T. announced. "Now I just have to get them wrapped and in the basement for the winter. Took me a while, but I got the job done. No help from you," she added gruffly, but Addie saw the twinkle in the old woman's bright blue eyes.

"Sorry," she grinned. "I'll help you put them out again next spring," she promised. "Where's Amy?" The Oldsmobile was not in its customary spot by the house.

"Took the car to town to pick up her sister. I guess she's coming for supper tonight."

"Amy's sister is coming here?"

Miss T. nodded. "Why should that surprise you?"

Addie shrugged. "I don't know. I guess I thought she didn't have any family close by. I mean, why . . ." she stopped.

"Why else would she take a job and live with me, when she's old enough to be retired herself and with her family?" Miss T. had an uncanny way of putting all the right words in your mouth, and this time was no exception. "I don't know the answer to that. And it's really none of my business. None of yours, either, miss."

She paused long enough to finish wrapping newspaper around some bulbs. She handed the bundle to Addie and nodded toward the wire basket behind the girl. Addie took the bundle and dropped it obediently in the basket.

"However, I'm certainly glad she did."

"Me, too." Addie waited for the next bundle of bulbs and placed them on top of the first.

"So. Why the gloomy face today?" Miss T. asked. She stopped wrapping bulbs and tipped Addie's chin back with a slightly dirty forefinger. "What's the problem? Where are the boys?"

Addie made a face at the smell of dirt and grass on Miss T.'s hand. The old woman wiped it on her equally dirty shirt. "Sorry."

"That's okay," Addie smiled. "Nick and Brian went to town with Nick's folks to see a movie. I don't care about that."

"Well, you obviously care about something and you're not going to feel better until you tell me what it is, so out with it."

Addie sighed. "I'm mad."

"At who?"

"Me."

"Whatever for?" Miss T. sat back on her heels and gave Addie a puzzled look.

"I lost my temper yesterday with Hillary ... a girl I thought was a friend. I don't know her very well, but she goes to my church and I thought she was ..." Addie stopped, not sure Miss T. would understand the difference between going to church and being a Christian.

"You thought she was a Christian." Evidently Miss T. understood the difference.

Addie nodded.

"But her behavior has been decidedly un-Christian."

"That's an understatement," Addie fumed. "She's been mean to Brian from the very first day of school. She teases him about something every chance she gets."

"How does Brian react?"

"He doesn't! He just takes it. He doesn't get angry. He doesn't even try to get back at her."

"So Brian acts more like a Christian than the Christian does."

"Brian *is* a Christian."

That took Miss T. by surprise. "What does Mr. Brady think of that?" she asked.

"He's still in shock," Addie admitted with a laugh.

"I'll bet," Miss T. replied. "Won't hurt him, though."

Addie shook her head in wonder. "You don't miss much, do you?"

"Hmpfh," Miss T. said. "I may be old, but I still have two eyes in my head. Just what did you say to Hillary?"

Addie was embarrassed. "I told her not to bother—"

"Speak up, child. Even someone with two good ears couldn't hear you mumbling like that."

"I told her she shouldn't bother to come to church if she's not going to listen to what's being taught."

Miss T.'s eyebrows shot up but, "My, oh my," was all she said. A minute or two passed while she continued wrapping bulbs in newspapers and handing the bundles to Addie. Finally she spoke.

"It would seem to me you need to apologize to Hillary and ask for her forgiveness."

"She needs to ask Brian for his forgiveness!" Addie protested.

"That's her decision to make. Asking for her forgiveness is yours."

"What if I ask for her forgiveness and she still treats Brian badly?"

Miss T. shrugged. "You've done what you know is right. You're not responsible for her actions."

"You sound like my father," Addie grumbled.

Miss T. smiled. "Thank you. I believe that's a compliment."

They finished wrapping and packing bulbs in companionable silence. When they were done, Addie dusted off her hands and picked up her bike.

"I'll talk to Hillary tomorrow," she promised Miss T.

"Good girl." Miss T. shaded her eyes to look down the road. "Is that my car? I believe it is. And I'm a mess. What a way to meet Amy's sister. I'd better get cleaned up. Goodbye, dear."

Miss T. hurried up the front steps and inside. Addie decided to wait and meet Amy's sister before she left. Amy pulled the Buick into the drive and parked next to the house.

The driver's door opened and Amy stepped out. She smiled at Addie, but her smile was strained. Another woman stepped from the back seat of the car and nodded politely as Amy made the introductions.

"Addie, this is my sister, Kimiko Tanaka. Kimi-san, this is my friend Addie."

Before Addie could speak, the passenger's door opened and Mr. Yamada emerged. He was even tinier than Addie remembered, but his sour expression had not changed. He acknowledged Addie with a brief nod and started toward the house.

"Come," he ordered without looking over his shoulder. "We have much to discuss."

Amy and Kimiko exchanged glances, then fell obediently into step behind the old man.

CHAPTER 9

Nosy Nick

Addie jumped from the car and ran up the Bradys' front steps. She knocked sharply and Brian answered the door.

"Are you ready?" she asked. Brian shook his head and gestured at the mild chaos going on in the room behind him.

Nick sat on the couch, trying to put socks and shoes on Jesse Kate. The toddler alternated between smacking Nick on the nose and pulling her socks off as fast as Nick got them on.

Mrs. Brady hopped across the room on one foot as she put on first one heel and then the other. Mr. Brady, an older version of Nick, stood in front of the dining room mirror, muttering under his breath as he yanked at his tie.

"Addie's here," Mrs. Brady said with a warning smile to Mr. Brady as his mutterings grew louder. "You'll have to excuse this bedlam, Addie. We haven't been to church in years, so we're just not used to getting everyone up and dressed and out the door on a Sunday morning."

She swooped Jesse Kate off of Nick's lap. "I'll put her shoes on in the car, Nick. Your tie looks fine, dear. Where are the car keys? Oh, here they are. All right everybody, let's go!"

Nick and his father exchanged baleful glances, but followed Mrs. Brady obediently out the door. Brian gave Addie a huge grin. "This should be interesting. See you there."

Bible class was first and the three older children trooped down the basement steps to the sixth grade room. Most of the class were already there, including Hillary Jackson and Mariel Cramer. Mariel gave them an embarrassed smile, but Hillary refused to look up when they entered the room.

She's not going to make this easy, Addie thought. *I'm going to get it over with right away, so I don't lose my nerve.*

"I'll be right back," she whispered to Nick.

Addie perched on the edge of the chair next to Hillary. "Hillary, I'm...Hillary?" The other girl looked up. The cold glare in her eyes made Addie shiver, but she plunged on. "I want to apologize for what I said to you Friday. I'm the one who needs to listen to what's being taught. Will you forgive me?"

Hillary glanced away for several seconds. When she looked back, Addie could see some of her anger had subsided. Still, she said nothing, only shrugged and nodded.

Addie took a deep breath and stood up. "Thanks," she said. She walked quickly back to her seat by Nick and Brian. Her spirit felt much lighter, even though Hillary had reacted just the way Addie suspected she would.

"What was that all about?" Nick asked, but Addie said nothing.

The hour passed quickly and their teacher asked Addie to say the closing prayer. She prayed willingly, thanking God for the important things they had learned from His Word.

"And thank you most of all for the forgiveness we all have because Your Son died for our sins. In His Name we pray, Amen." Amens echoed around the room. Mariel's was the loudest and she stopped Addie and the boys before they could get out of the room.

"Hi, Brian. Hi, Nick. Did you come with Addie today? I'm glad you came. I hope you're not mad at me, Brian. I didn't want everyone to tease you about being a brain on Friday. I just thought since Nick called you 'brain,' it was your nickname or something. It fits, don't you think? I mean, you are a brain, you know..."

Mariel's voice droned on all the way upstairs, and Brian was polite enough to listen. Addie and Nick could barely control their laughter at the brief uh-huhs and huh-uhs Brian was able to inject into the lop-sided conversation.

Mariel followed them into the sanctuary and down the aisle. Amy and her sister sat in the pew with Addie and Nick's parents, so the children took seats behind them. Mariel stepped over the boys' legs to sit next to Addie. Hillary walked slowly down the aisle and Mariel patted the space next to her. When Hillary hesitated, Addie smiled and nodded. Hillary smiled a tight little smile and sat down.

The service was a lively one, with lots of singing. Jesse Kate added a variety of sound effects, especially when she discovered her older brother sitting directly behind her. She gurgled, blew bubbles, played peek-a-boo, and occasionally drowned out the elder with her high-pitched squeals.

After one particularly ear-shattering note, Mr. Brady reached over and gave the little girl a gentle pat on the leg. It couldn't have hurt, but it served its purpose. Jesse Kate stuck out her lower lip and plopped down on the floor, where she curled up and promptly fell asleep.

Things proceeded quietly after that and even Nick enjoyed the message that was given. "Short but sweet," he whispered in Addie's ear.

Worship time ended with Addie's favorite song. The words alone gave "Blow a Trumpet in Zion" a powerful message, but when Nate Bates played the trumpet solo at the end, Addie always got goose bumps. She prayed God would let her sit in Mr. Bates' section of heaven some day.

Announcements came last and were almost finished when Hillary giggled softly. All the other kids leaned over to see what she was staring at.

Evidently the trumpet solo had awakened Jesse Kate. Unbeknownst to her parents, she had crawled under the pews and now sat at the feet of Mr. Bates, who had not yet noticed the little girl. She held his trumpet awkwardly and had most of her face in the bell. Her lips were pursed and she was blowing softly.

When that didn't work, she attempted to turn the trumpet around, but only succeeded in bonking herself in the head and toppling over. All the children erupted into giggles which finally got the attention of the rest of the congregation. Hillary was closest, so she jumped up to help the little girl. Nick was right behind her and together they managed to loosen the trumpet from the toddler's grasp. Nick carried her back to his parents amid much laughter.

After the service, Hillary stopped Addie and the boys at the back door. "I'm sorry too, Addie," she murmured. She swallowed hard and looked at Brian. "I'm glad you came today. Both of you," she added hastily when Nick sniffed.

"Thanks," said Brian. "See you tomorrow."

Hillary nodded. "Right. Bye." She turned and hurried out the door.

"We'll see how she acts at school," Nick said. His expression clearly showed he was not ready to believe Hillary's change of heart.

"Give her a chance, Nick," Addie admonished him. Nick only shrugged so Addie changed the subject. "Did you guys know we're going out to lunch together?"

Nick grimaced. "Yeah, the Golden Creek restaurant. It's going to be a lot of fun chasing Jesse Kate around that fancy place."

As it turned out, the toddler was tired from her trip to church and fell asleep in Mr. Brady's arms while they waited for their table. That gave Addie, Nick and Brian a chance to talk quietly on an ornate wooden bench set in front of a row of tall, potted plants.

"You'll never guess who I met yesterday," Addie said softly. "I've been dying to tell you all morning."

"Who?" Nick pushed away the leaves of the plant behind him that were tickling his neck.

"Kimiko Tanaka. Amy's sister."

"Oh." Nick was clearly disappointed. "So what?"

"Amy invited her out for supper, but when she got home, she had Mr. Yamada with her as well. I didn't even get to talk to Amy's sister. Mr. Yamada said they had 'much to discuss,' so they all went inside."

The two boys listened to this news and Brian frowned. "I sure wish we knew what was going on."

"You can bet they were talking about whatever Mr. Yamada thinks will disgrace Amy's family. Why else would her sister be there?" Nick said.

Addie nodded. "That's what I thought, too. But I don't know how we can find out anything else, unless we come right out and ask Amy."

"It's probably none of our business, anyway," Brian said.

"I'm sure Amy can take care of herself and her family just fine," Addie agreed.

"It would be rude to ask Amy about it," Nick added.

Suddenly Brian sat up very straight and his brown eyes widened. "Maybe we won't have to," he whispered. "Listen."

From the other side of the potted plants, the children could hear another conversation. As they listened, the voices grew louder. Nick squirmed around on the bench and gently pushed back the leaves of the small tree, trying to see through the green maze. Suddenly he broke into a big grin.

"You're right," he whispered to Brian. "It's Yamada and his driver." Then his grin faded. "They're speaking Japanese," he whispered.

"Give me a piece of paper and a pencil, Addie." Brian's request was soft but urgent and Addie dug through her purse for a pencil. The only paper she had was the bulletin from church but it was enough. Brian grabbed it and scribbled a few words around the border of the Scripture lesson for the day.

Suddenly the voices dropped dramatically and Brian stopped writing. Nick pushed the branches aside once more, but the conversation behind them was still inaudible. Nick turned around on his knees and cautiously tried to separate two of the large clay pots that held the plants. He tottered on the edge of the bench and one of the pots began to tip.

"Watch out, Nick," Addie hissed, but it was too late. The pot tipped over and Nick lost his balance, tumbling through the plants and over the bench on the other side, landing squarely at the feet of a very surprised Mr. Yamada.

CHAPTER 10

The Japan House

In the commotion that followed, Addie managed to slip quietly to her parents' side and out of view of Mr. Yamada. She didn't know if he would recognize her, but she didn't want to take that risk.

Brian helped Nick to his feet and together they picked up the fallen plant. The manager had arrived by then and was directing the cleanup while Nick's parents apologized profusely to the elderly Japanese man. He was still seated on the bench, emptying his shoes of dirt.

"There is no problem. I am fine," was his terse reply to Nick's mumbled "I'm sorry, sir.'" The younger Japanese man smiled and made polite conversation with the family while the mess was cleared away. Fortunately, at that moment the hostess called, "McCormick, party of eight." Another woman came to escort Mr. Yamada and his friend to their table. Addie noticed they were seated on opposite sides of the restaurant.

"For heaven's sake, Nick, sit still," commanded Mrs. Brady, as the children took seats at one end of the long table.

Addie tried to keep the giggle out of her voice. "I think I'll sit next to Brian."

"Be quiet," Nick growled. "Did you understand anything he said?" he asked Brian.

Brian shook his head. "The only words I'm sure of were words that were repeated several times. And I don't know what they mean. I'll have to look them up when we get home."

He shoved the bulletin at Addie and Nick. Yoshiosan, knockama, and soupeye were scrawled around the edge of the paper. "As far as I could tell, Mr. Yamada kept saying Yoshiosan knockama. But his friend disagreed with him, and kept saying Yoshiosan soupeye." He took the paper back and studied the words again. "I know these are spelled incorrectly. I wrote down what I heard, but I have no idea how to spell them in Japanese."

"Who else do we know that speaks Japanese, besides Amy?" Addie asked.

"My dad," Brian replied. "But I don't think your folks would want me to make a long distance call to Japan just to ask him what three words mean."

Nick nodded his head in agreement and the three children were quiet as a waiter brought a large bowl of lettuce with a tray of vegetables to their table. They fixed their own salads and ate in silence. Jesse Kate was awake again and amused herself by tossing croutons at them down the table.

Suddenly Addie snapped her fingers. "This is a university town! Surely there's a department we can call that will translate these words for us."

"They're not spelled right, Addie," Nick reminded her.

"They don't have to be spelled right," she replied. "Do you think you can pronounce them correctly?" she asked Brian.

He hesitated, then nodded. "Close enough, anyway. But we'll have to wait until tomorrow. I'm sure there's no one there today."

"No one where?" asked Mrs. Brady. She was wiping off Jesse Kate's fingers and retrieving croutons up and down the table and heard Brian's last comment.

Brian coughed. "Uh, at one of the departments here at the university. The Japanese department. We're interested in some of the things Amy's told us and we had some questions."

"Why not ask Amy?" Mrs. Brady replied sensibly.

Nick answered. "I'd like to learn more about bonsai, Mom. You know, those plants that look like miniature trees. I bet the library here has lots of books on the subject."

"Do you like the art of bonsai, Nick?" Mrs. McCormick was listening to the conversation now. "The Japan House has some beautiful bonsai in their garden. Amy took me on a personal tour once. She volunteers there one Saturday a month. I'm sure she'd be glad to take you sometime."

"Could we go today, Mom?" Addie asked. "We're not doing anything this afternoon, are we?"

"Well," Mrs. McCormick hesitated, then smiled at her daughter's eager face. "Let's ask your father."

"Ask me what?" Mr. McCormick said between bites of his steak.

"Could we drive by The Japan House on our way home this afternoon? The kids would like to see it . . . if that's all right with you," she said to Mrs. Brady.

Mrs. Brady moved quickly to prevent Jesse Kate from sticking her hand in the salad dressing. "If you don't mind taking them, I'd appreciate it," she said. "We need to get Jesse home for her nap. I could use one myself," she added with a tired sigh as she wiped bleu cheese from between the little girl's fingers.

Mr. McCormick agreed to the trip as well. With that settled, the McCormicks and the Bradys finished lunch and parted company soon afterward.

Mr. McCormick found The Japan House after only two wrong turns. When they finally arrived at their destination, the house appeared empty. Bamboo curtains covered all the windows and no one was in sight.

The children were disappointed and Mr. McCormick was going to drive past, but Mrs. McCormick stopped him.

"I'm sure we can get in. The brother and sister who run the house live here. Amy told me they prefer to take appointments, but they never turn anyone away. It can't hurt to try, right?"

"Right," all three children chorused, so Mr. McCormick pulled into the driveway.

No one answered the door, but Mrs. McCormick motioned them around the side of the house. There they found a gate that adjoined a fence which surrounded the property. She lifted the latch and glanced in. Soon the gate opened all the way and they were met by a beautiful young Japanese woman dressed in a dramatic red and gold kimono. She bowed politely.

Mrs. McCormick introduced herself and her husband, then the children.

"My name is Sagiri," the woman said. "May I offer you *o-cha*? Tea," she translated with a smile.

"No, thank you. We just finished lunch," said Mrs. McCormick. "We're friends of Amy Takahashi. I've been here before, but the children haven't and they were especially interested in seeing your garden."

At the mention of Amy's name, the woman's smile deepened. "I will be happy to show you what you wish to see and answer any questions you have. My brother is with another visitor inside right now, but he will be out shortly. Please, come in."

Sagiri allowed them to wander through the delicate, well-kept garden, speaking only when they had questions. Soon they were joined by her brother, Masao. After brief introductions, Nick managed to draw Mr. and Mrs. McCormick's attention to the variety of bonsai plants at the rear of the garden. This left Addie and Brian alone with Masao and Sagiri.

Addie started the conversation. "Brian's father lives in Japan. His company sent him there to set up their restaurant chain. Brian's going to be leaving soon to join him."

"That is wonderful," Sagiri said. "I think you will find our country a very exciting place to visit."

Brian nodded. "I'm looking forward to it. Amy is helping me with the language—nothing formal, just some of the phrases and expressions I'll need to get around at first. I'm able to pick out words in a conversation, but I don't know enough to know what they mean yet."

"What were those words you were telling us about today?" Addie asked innocently.

Brian repeated the words in halting Japanese and Sagiri smiled. "It sounds as if you were watching a Japanese spy movie," she laughed. "*Nakama* means 'insider' in Japanese. It implies a closeness and an intimacy with a group of people. Your family is one kind of nakama. *Supai* is what we call an import word. We have no equivalent in Japanese, so we adapted one of your words to fit our language." She repeated the word rapidly. "Supai. Supai means spy."

"What about yoshiosan?" Brian asked.

"That is . . ."

"That is a name." Masao interrupted his sister, and for the first time, Addie and Brian noticed the deep frown that furrowed his brow. Masao was staring at them intently. "Yoshio is a man's name. San is an honorary term that is added to a name out of respect, or when the person speaking is a close friend."

Addie tried to sort out the meaning of what Brian had heard that afternoon. Mr. Yamada seemed to believe Yoshiosan was an insider, but his driver thought he was a spy. Was that it? Or was it the other way around? And who was Yoshiosan? Suddenly the name clicked. *Yoshio Nomura. Amy's father. Amy's father was a spy!?*

Addie looked quickly at Brian to see if he had made the same connection, but Brian's attention was elsewhere. Addie followed his gaze and saw Mr. Yamada's driver staring at them out the back window of The Japan House.

CHAPTER 11

Current Events

Masao watched Addie's reaction out of the corner of his eye. After another minute or two of polite conversation, he excused himself and hurried inside.

"Do you know our visitor?" Sagiri asked Addie quietly.

Addie shook her head. "Not really. We've seen him with another man at Amy's, but we've never met him."

Sagiri's troubled eyes studied the now-empty window. "Mr. Yamada," she said.

Addie nodded.

Sagiri was silent. Nick saw that they had finished talking and he walked Mr. and Mrs. McCormick back to the rest of the group.

"Please greet Amiko-san for me. I always enjoy the time we spend together each month," Sagiri said. "I look forward to your return as well. Perhaps we can persuade you to have o-cha on your next visit," she smiled.

"What were you talking about with Sagiri?" Mr. McCormick asked Addie on the way home.

Addie sighed and Nick shook his head. It was impossible to keep anything from her father for very long.

"Go ahead and tell him," Nick said softly. "Maybe he can help."

Addie took a deep breath and began. "We were talking about Mr. Yamada. He was at The Japan House while we were in the garden."

"The man from the restaurant? I didn't see him."

"We didn't either, but his driver was inside."

"What driver? How do you know all this?" Mr. McCormick gave his daughter a curious glance in the rear-view mirror.

"We've met Mr. Yamada before. He's been to visit Amy a couple of times," Addie answered.

"I see." Mr. McCormick relaxed. "I'm surprised he didn't recognize you, Nick."

"I think he did," Nick muttered.

"He certainly didn't act like . . . wait a minute. Why don't I like the sound of this? What are you kids getting into now? That *was* an accident at the restaurant, wasn't it?"

"It sure was," Nick said emphatically. "I didn't mean to get caught."

Mrs. McCormick turned around and gave Nick an astonished look. "Were you eavesdropping?"

Nick's tell-tale blush gave him away and Mrs. McCormick turned to her daughter. "Addie," she began.

"We haven't done a thing, Mom," Addie said before she could continue. "We've just been in the right places at the right times."

"Or the wrong places at the wrong times," her father said. "What's up, kiddo?"

"Mr. Yamada is bothering Amy. He's convinced their families are going to be disgraced, but she doesn't agree."

"You have no idea what the problem is?"

Brian took over the story. "We didn't, at least not until today. Now we think it has something to do with Amy's father. He was a famous artist. Amy has a lot of his paintings in her room."

"When we heard Yamada and his driver talking in the restaurant today, we wanted to see if they were talking about Amy," Nick said.

Mr. McCormick frowned. "I heard them talking too. It was all Japanese. Since when do you understand Japanese, Nick?"

Nick grinned. "I don't. Brian does."

"No, I don't," Brian protested. "But I could pick out some of the words they were saying, and I wrote them down."

Mrs. McCormick finished the story for them. "Of course, you couldn't ask Amy to translate them for you, so you talked us into visiting The Japan House." She and Mr. McCormick exchanged glances, but Addie could tell they were trying not to smile.

"So what were the words?" Mr. McCormick asked.

"Yoshio-san, nakama, and supai." Brian recited the list in his best Japanese accent. Addie giggled.

"English, please," Mr. McCormick said wryly.

"Oh." Brian blushed, but grinned. "Sorry. Yoshio-san is a name."

"Amy's father's name was Yoshio," Nick interrupted.

"Nakama means insider, and supai means spy," Brian finished.

Mr. and Mrs. McCormick exchanged another glance, this one much more serious.

"I know that Amy and her family spent most of the war years in a relocation center after Pearl Harbor was bombed," Mrs. McCormick said.

"Why did they put Japanese in prison camps, anyway?" Nick asked.

"When Japan attacked American soil, the government became very suspicious of all Japanese," Brian replied. "They wanted to make sure no one was leaking information that could lead to an attack on the continental United States."

"Right, Brian," said Mr. McCormick. "It was unfortunate, because the Japanese were model citizens. There were never any Japanese convicted of espionage."

"I wonder what makes Mr. Yamada think Amy's father was a spy?" Nick questioned.

"Oh, he doesn't," Brian said hastily. "It's that other guy, his driver. He's the one who kept saying Yoshio-san supai."

"Why would it matter to his driver?" Addie mused.

"Maybe he's not just a driver," Mr. McCormick offered. "Whoever he is, I'm glad you haven't taken matters into your own hands. If Amy needs any help, I think she knows enough to ask."

"It sounds to me as if this is a personal matter," Mrs. McCormick added. "Honor and family are very important to the Japanese. If there is disgrace in a family, they don't like to talk about it. If Amy wants to keep it private, let her." Mrs. McCormick's tone was soft, but there was a warning note in her voice and the children knew she meant it.

Well, that's that, Addie thought with some disappointment.

At least, that was that until the next morning at school. Mrs. Himmel had designated Monday as "Current Events Day," and they began by reading through the copies of the Sunday paper they were required to bring from home.

"I don't want to make a habit of starting with the 'Arts and Entertainment' section," Mrs. Himmel said. "On the other hand, I believe in reinforcing any student who takes the initiative of reading the paper and investigating subjects that are of interest to him." She paused and looked at Brian.

"Brian, Mrs. Hilst told me you were looking for information on the paintings of Yoshio Nomura last week. Would you please tell us what you've found out about him, and why his name has been in the newspaper this last week?"

Brian's face went blank, and he opened and closed his mouth twice. He recovered enough to thumb through his paper and pull out the "Arts and Entertainment" section.

Addie followed suit and her eyes widened at what she saw. In the lower right hand corner was a small but recognizable picture. It was a pencil drawing of three little girls in a garden.

CHAPTER 12

Hillary's Hunch

Fortunately, another of Brian's seemingly unlimited talents was speedreading. He skimmed the article in record time and summarized what he knew.

"Yoshio Nomura is...well, was...a famous Japanese artist. He was taken to the relocation center at Manzanar with his family after the bombing of Pearl Harbor during World War II. The paintings he did of that time became real valuable. Most of them are in museums or private collections in Japan, but some of them have disappeared. Most people believe they're in the private collections of his family." Brian took a deep breath, and pointed to the paper in front of him.

"This is a sketch they found in the personal effects of his nephew after his nephew died last month. It's important because no one knew Nomura made preliminary sketches of his paintings."

Addie finished reading the article just as Brian ended his explanation. She glanced at Nick, but he was still reading. Brian looked up to see Addie watching him, and shrugged his shoulders slightly. Nick finished and flopped back in his chair with a huge sigh.

"That's not quite the whole story, Brian. Does anyone want to add anything?"

Hillary raised her hand. "It says the sketch and the painting have the same subject—three little girls—but the backgrounds are different. In the sketch all you see is dirt and a barbed wire fence. But the painting has the little girls playing in a beautiful garden."

"That's right," Mrs. Himmel said. "Brian, did you ever see a picture of this painting?"

Brian nodded and lifted the lid to his desk. He pulled out the huge book he had shown Addie and Nick the week before and opened it to the painting.

"Why don't you pass that around so we can all see the differences?"

Brian handed it to the boy in front of him, and the book slowly progressed around the room. Addie and Hillary looked at the picture together, comparing the sketch in the newspaper to the finished painting. Not only had the background changed, but the children's clothes were different as well. In the sketch, the little girls were dressed in ragged, patched shirts and pants. In the painting, their kimonos were bright and beautiful.

"Why do you think there's such a difference between the sketch and the painting?" Mrs. Himmel asked.

One boy raised his hand. "Who would want to buy a picture of three grubby little kids playing in the dirt?"

There was a spattering of laughter and Mrs. Himmel smiled. "The painting is definitely more pleasing to the eye, isn't it? Any other reason? Yes, Mariel?"

"My uncle does that all the time," Mariel began. "He's a painter and he travels all over the country taking pictures of scenery and people that he thinks would look good in a painting. Then he comes home and paints pictures of people and places that might be 200 miles apart in real life. He says that's the way he wants to paint it, so . . ."

"All right," Mrs. Himmel interrupted smoothly. "An artist has freedom of expression, doesn't he? There's not a law that says he has to paint exactly what he sees. Can anyone think of any other reasons? Brian?"

Brian had not raised his hand, but he did have an answer. "Maybe he sketched what he saw, but he painted what he wanted to see."

"Say what?" came a voice from the back and several students snickered.

"Wait a minute." Mrs. Himmel raised her hand for quiet. "I think Brian has a point. Does anyone want to expand on that? Yes, Hillary."

Hillary lowered her hand and spoke slowly. "I think I know what Brian means. The caption under the painting said the three girls were Nomura's daughters. He drew the sketch while they were in the relocation center. It must have been hard for him to watch his daughters grow up in such an ugly place. When he painted the picture, maybe he painted the background he wanted for them, one that was beautiful and secure."

There was silence when she finished and Mrs. Himmel gave a satisfied nod. "Very good, Hillary. Is that what you meant, Brian?"

Brian nodded and he and Hillary exchanged a friendly glance.

"Of course, we will never know Nomura's exact reasons for changing the painting, but I think you've all offered some logical explanations. Now, let's go back to the front page..."

"So do we still mind our own business?" Nick asked at morning break. Addie didn't answer and Brian shook his head. "I don't know. What if Amy has more sketches like that one?"

Addie and Nick exchanged a surprised look. "I guess we never told you, did we?" Addie said. "I almost forgot about it myself until now."

"Told me what?"

"She's got a whole book of sketches!" Nick exclaimed.

"What?" Brian almost shouted.

"The first day we went to visit Amy—you weren't here yet—Nick opened a scrapbook sitting on her table. It was full of sketches just like the one in the newspaper today," Addie said.

Nick finished the story. "She got real upset when I opened it. She locked it in a drawer in her desk and we haven't seen it since."

"No wonder Mr. Yamada won't leave her alone," Brian said. "He wants to get his hands on those sketches. Can you imagine how much they're worth?"

They sat silently contemplating the possible wealth locked away in Amy's desk. Just then Hillary walked up.

"Hi," she said awkwardly.

Only Addie responded. "Hi, Hillary."

"I think it's great you're going to Japan, Brian." Hillary blushed when Nick sniffed loudly. "I don't mean I'm glad you're leaving. I just think it would be fun to go to another country."

Brian kicked Nick's shoe and frowned at him. "It should be fun."

"I was really surprised to see that picture in the paper today," Hillary continued. "I have a friend who has a copy of that painting. She has the whole series, in fact."

Suddenly, Addie's stomach dropped down to her toes. Hillary went to her church. Amy went to her church. Did Hillary know Amy?

"Who's that?" Brian tried to keep his voice casual, but Addie heard the tension in it.

"She goes to our church," Hillary answered. "I think Addie knows her too. Amy Takahashi."

Addie swallowed and nodded. "How did you see her paintings?" she asked.

"Last summer...not this past summer, but a year ago...she and I were both volunteers at your dad's radio station. I guess it wasn't your dad's yet, was it? Anyway, we worked the same hours and I'd walk home with her. She only lived a block from my grandma. She's got some beautiful things from Japan. You'd love them, Brian."

Brian nodded. "I've seen them. I've met Amy, too."

"How—?"

Addie spoke up. "Amy works as a live-in companion for a friend of my family's now. Miss T.'s house is about a mile away from Nick and I, so we visit them a lot."

Hillary made the connection immediately. "Now I get it! That's why you were so interested in Nomura. You saw his paintings at Amy's!"

No one said anything, but Hillary heard her answer in their silence. Her quick mind worked so fast Addie could practically see wheels turning and hear bells ringing.

"Are those paintings originals?" she asked. Still no answer.

"How could Amy afford original paintings like those?" No answer. "Amy once told me she had to live in a relocation center when she was little. Maybe she met Nomura there!"

Hillary was getting close to the truth fast, and there was nothing any of them could do about it but keep quiet. But their silence only fed the other girl's imagination. She watched their faces closely and when Nick winced at her last statement, she knew she was on to something. She frowned, thinking hard, and suddenly the truth settled over her like a soft blanket. All the color drained from her face. When she spoke again it was almost a whisper.

"Is Amy one of the girls in the painting?"

The answer stared back at her from three pairs of eyes.

CHAPTER 13

The Scrapbook Revealed

"It's none of your business, Hillary, so just butt out!" Nick's rude outburst shocked everyone, but Brian recovered first.

"Stop it, Nick," he warned. Addie had never heard that tone of voice from Brian. Tension hung over them for several seconds, and finally Nick backed down.

"I just don't trust her," he grumbled.

"I'm not stupid, Nick." Hillary's anger was apparent, but she managed to keep her voice calm. "I know this is serious. If you think I'd ever do anything to hurt Amy, you're wrong." She turned to Brian. "Is Amy one of the girls in the painting?"

He nodded.

Hillary was puzzled. "Why has she kept that a secret for so long?"

She looked from Brian to Addie. Both of them looked at Nick, but he was busy digging circles in the dirt with the toe of his shoe and refused to look up.

Finally Brian spoke. "We heard something yesterday that might explain why."

"Brian!" Nick was furious but Brian ignored his protest.

"There are some people who believe Amy's father might have been a spy in World War II."

Hillary nodded. "Artists were always suspect in times of war. Giving someone a work of art was a good cover for transferring secret information." She spoke with such authority the other three looked at her in surprise. "That's how they did it in the movies," she said lamely.

"Why didn't I think of that?" Brian said. "It sounds kind of corny, but it makes sense. Nomura could have been passing information to his countrymen through his art. Your father said there were never any Japanese convicted of espionage, but now that this sketch has been found, people are bound to start talking again. At least Mr. Yamada thinks they will."

"Of course!" Addie interrupted. "Remember what he said the first time we saw him at Amy's? He said, 'Please tell me where they are.' He probably meant the other sketches. He tried to convince Amy her family was going to be disgraced if she didn't tell him. Then we heard his driver call 'Yoshio-san' a 'supai'—a spy."

"Who's Mr. Yamada?" Hillary asked.

"A man Amy knows," Addie replied.

"It sounds like Mr. Yamada thinks more of these sketches will show up and prove that 'Yoshio-san' was a spy," Nick summarized, his anger gone for the moment. "That would explain why Amy won't show anyone the scrapbook."

"What scrapbook?" Hillary didn't miss a thing!

Nick groaned. "Me and my mouth."

Brian smiled. "It's okay, Nick. We might as well tell her everything. She's already helped us make more sense out of all this."

"Amy has a scrapbook full of sketches like the one in the newspaper," Addie explained to Hillary.

"We should go to see Amy today," Brian decided. "If we take the picture from the newspaper, maybe she'll be willing to tell us about it. We could tell her what we know about Mr. Yamada. If she doesn't want to talk about it, at least we'll know we tried."

"I'll pray for you," Hillary said shyly. "I hope nothing bad comes out of all this. Amy's so nice. It's hard to believe her father was a spy."

"We're not sure he was," Brian reminded her.

"Right." Hillary nodded. "I hope he wasn't, for Amy's sake." She looked at Nick. "You don't have to worry. I won't tell anyone about this. I *can* be trusted." She turned and walked away.

"Why'd you have to tell her, Brian?" Nick demanded when Hillary was out of earshot. "If I didn't know better, I'd think you were trying to make up to her!"

"What's wrong with that?" Brian's patience snapped, but he apologized immediately. "I'm sorry, Nick. You're right. I *was* trying to make up to Hillary. I don't like coming to school every day, wondering what she's going to say or do next. I'm only going to be here three months. I don't want to spend the whole time avoiding her. I'd rather enjoy myself."

Nick was silent. Finally he mumbled, "I never thought of it that way. Sorry."

"It's okay," Brian said. "Let's forget it."

Mrs. Himmel called them back to class and the rest of the morning passed quickly. After school, Addie hurried out to the bus yard in order to get a seat next to Brian and Nick. Mariel was sitting in the seat in front of them, waiting for her.

"Hi, Addie, I saved you a seat. Say, I saw you talking to HIllary at break this morning. I'm glad you're friends again, aren't you, Addie? Hillary's really nice. I know you guys will like her if you give her a chance. Sometimes she talks and says things she shouldn't, but I guess we all do that, don't we?"

Mariel carried on her monologue until the bus thundered to a stop at her corner. She chattered all the way out the door. "See you in the morning. Save me a seat, okay, Addie . . . ?"

Addie leaned against the window and stretched her legs out over the worn leather seat. Nick and Brian both relaxed and the bus was infinitely quieter.

"You know," Nick commented, "someone ought to tell Mariel how rude she can be."

Brian and Addie both looked at Nick and the memory of his earlier conversation with Hillary came flooding back. He pinked up considerably just at the thought and grinned sheepishly. "Probably not me, though, right?"

Addie and Brian both laughed. The bus down-shifted and groaned around the corner that led to Nick's house. Suddenly, Addie snapped her fingers. "Did anyone remember the picture from the newspaper? I forgot mine."

"I've got it," Brian said.

"Brian the brain," Nick teased. "Always prepared."

Brian grinned back. "That's me."

"It doesn't bother you to be called 'the brain?'" Addie asked.

"Nah," Brian said. "I've been called that all my life."

"What?" Addie exclaimed.

"Yeah," Brian nodded. "It bothered you two a lot more than it did me when Mariel started that. In France they called me *Monsieur l'intelligent*. I'm used to it."

Nick was indignant. "I almost got in a fight defending you! And you didn't even care? Thanks a lot, pal!"

"Hey, I figured maybe someone would pound some sense into you," Brian teased and Nick pummelled his arm mercilessly until the bus screeched to a standstill in front of the Bradys'.

"I'll be down in five minutes," Addie called after them as they bounded down the steps.

There were several cars on the country road, so they rode single file to Miss T.'s house. Brian was first, Addie next and Nick trailed behind. Brian was the first to see the car pull out of Miss T.'s driveway.

"Look," he called to the other two. A red car approached them and as it passed they all saw the stern countenance of Mr. Yamada on the passenger's side. His driver gave them a brief nod, but Yamada stared straight ahead.

As soon as the car had passed, Nick pulled around Addie and stood up to pedal. "Let's move!" he shouted.

They arrived at Miss T.'s breathless. None of them felt right walking in the front door unannounced, but Addie and Nick had no reservations about slipping in the back without an invitation. Miss T. had made it clear they were welcome in her kitchen anytime.

Now she was sitting at the table peeling apples. She beckoned them inside.

"Is Amy here?" Addie asked without even saying hello.

"What am I, chopped liver?" Miss T. often heard the children banter back and forth, and that particular expression was one of her favorites. Now she imitated Nick's gruff voice quite well and Brian laughed in spite of himself.

"Very funny," Nick muttered, but he grinned at the elderly woman and she motioned down the hall to Amy's room.

"Take a number and get in line," she said. "There have been people in and out of this house all day. Mr. Yamada just left and now another sister is here to visit her."

"Another sister?" all three children chorused and Miss T. covered her ears.

"Don't do that," she grumbled, fiddling with her hearing aids. They heard a loud squawk from behind her ear and Addie shivered. "Just when I think I've got these blessed things adjusted, you all come along and start talking in three-part harmony. Now I have to readjust them."

They left Miss T. mumbling to herself and tapping her ear gently. They walked down the long hallway and Addie knocked at the door to Amy's room. It swung open silently and Amy looked up from the table in the middle of the room and smiled.

Amy's two sisters sat next to her. Addie was amazed at the likeness they still had to the paintings. The faces were older but the expressions were the same.

The scrapbook lay open on the table in front of them. A pencil drawing of the second painting in the series was on the right side of the book. On the left, where the first drawing should have been, was the ragged edge of a torn-out page.

CHAPTER 14

Three Sisters

"Please come in children." Amy rose gracefully from the floor. At the sight of her bare feet, Addie hastily removed her own shoes. Brian and Nick followed suit. They all stood just inside the doorway, trying to look anywhere but at the open scrapbook.

"These are my sisters, Kimiko and Marako," Amy said. She introduced the children and there were polite murmurs on both sides.

Brian cleared his throat and dug in his back pocket for the newspaper clipping. Amy stopped him when she saw the ragged paper.

"That is not necessary Brian," she said. "Several weeks ago, Oji-san told my sisters and I the missing sketch had been found." She turned to Addie and Nick. "Brian has never seen the scrapbook, but I am sure you and Nick made the connection."

Addie nodded. "I know it's probably none of our business, but we thought we should tell you what we know about Mr. Yamada."

Amy gave Addie a puzzled look and glanced back at her sisters. Kimiko tried to hide a smile. Amy motioned for the children to sit and the three of them took seats on the floor across from the two sisters.

"May I offer you some tea?" she asked politely.

"No, thanks." Nick was quick to refuse, but Addie and Brian both accepted the offer. Amy poured the steaming drink into two of her small lacquered cups.

"Perhaps a soft drink?" she suggested to Nick and he grinned.

"Now you're talking," he said.

Amy disappeared out the door and was back in seconds with a glass of ice and a can of soda. She poured the drink for Nick, then settled herself at the end of the table, between her sisters and the children.

"Now," Amy asked, "what do you know?"

"Not much, really," Brian said. "We saw Mr. Yamada at a restaurant yesterday. He and his driver were talking—in Japanese, of course—and I was able to pick out some of the words. I didn't know what they meant, so we asked Addie's folks to take us to The Japan House. Sagiri translated the words for us."

"And what were the words?" Marako spoke for the first time. Her question was a sad one, as if she knew the answer.

"Yoshio-san, nakama, supai." Brian's voice was very soft as he repeated the words in Japanese. All three sisters bowed their heads and Amy sighed audibly.

"We saw Mr. Yamada at The Japan House, too," Addie said. "When we read this article in the newspaper, we were afraid he was trying to find your scrapbook so he could sell the sketches . . . or prove your father was a spy." Addie stopped when Kimiko shook her head.

"No," the woman said quietly. "Oji-san wishes us no harm. He only wants to protect our family from disgrace. He knows one of us has the scrapbook. He has always insisted our father is innocent of all the accusations made against him. He believes the proof is in the scrapbook."

"What do you think?" Nick asked.

Amy shook her head. "I have looked through these pages many times, trying to find something that would prove his innocence. There is nothing." She sighed. "Kimiko and Marako have looked as well."

"Maybe you're looking for the wrong thing," Nick suggested.

"That is part of the problem," she agreed. "I do not know *what* I am looking for." She pulled the open scrapbook toward her and all three children leaned forward. She smiled at their curiosity.

"You know our family spent the war years at the relocation center in Manzanar," she said.

The children nodded.

"Our father spent much of his time there telling us stories and drawing pictures to illustrate them. This is the book that holds those pictures."

"After the war, he did many paintings of our life at Manzanar, but none of those sketches are here,"

Kimiko said. "The sketches that led to our paintings," she nodded to the series on the wall, "are the only ones from the scrapbook he finished."

Amy flipped through the book slowly. Each sister took turns pointing out her favorite story or explaining the significance of a particular picture.

"This is the story I remember most vividly," Amy said. The first picture she pointed to showed two richly dressed monarchs sitting on large chairs above a room full of people.

"The emperor and empress had many servants. One of them, the court musician, was a very gifted man. Other servants were jealous of him and accused him of playing his music for another master."

The next picture showed a man on his knees in front of the emperor. "He denied it, of course, but no one believed him. He was banished from the court and lived his life in exile in the mountains."

The last picture showed the musician playing his instrument on a deserted mountainside, while people in the valley looked up to listen. "There he continued to play, and the music once heard only by the emperor now lives forever in the hearts of the people."

"That's your father's story," Addie said softly.

Amy nodded. "But it is not proof of an innocent man."

"There are still those who wish to believe our father was a . . . spy." Marako found the word difficult to speak.

"Mr. Yamada's driver," Nick blurted and Amy nodded. "If Mr. Yamada thinks your father is innocent, why does he put up with that guy?" he asked bluntly.

"Kenji is his grandson," Amy answered gently.

"Oh."

" Mr. Yamada is our uncle," she finished.

Addie, Nick and Brian all stared at her. Finally Addie found her voice. "Your uncle?"

Amy nodded.

"Your father's brother?"

"No," said Kimiko. "Our mother's brother. However, my father had no brothers of his own and he considered Oji-san as close as a brother."

"If Mr. Yamada believes your father was innocent, why does his grandson want to prove otherwise?" Brian asked.

"That is difficult to explain," Amy answered. "Generations change. What was important to our parents is not so important to our children."

"Family honor is sacred to Oji-san," Marako continued. "Kenji is more concerned with money and possessions. If rumors of espionage will make our father's art more valuable, what is the harm? No one adheres to the traditional values any longer, at least no one in Kenji's generation."

"Perhaps we are being too harsh," Amy reproached her sister. "You know our own father did not find his security in the traditions of his ancestors. His security was found in the blood of Jesus Christ."

"Kenji does not adhere to those beliefs either," Marako reminded her.

"Your father was a Christian?" Brian asked with some surprise.

"Oh, yes," Amy smiled. "He accepted the Lord our first year at Manzanar. His faith led us to Jesus Christ. He gave us the strength to stand against the rejection we experienced because of the rumors."

"But he couldn't have been a spy if he was a Christian!" Addie exclaimed.

"You must remember we were relocated *after* of the bombing of Pearl Harbor. Oji-san believes it is possible my father had opportunities for espionage before he accepted Christ at Manzanar," Amy said.

"Why didn't you just *ask* him if he was a spy?" Nick wanted to know.

Kimiko smiled. "Even in the closest Japanese families, there was a respect for elders that kept a distance between them and their children. We would never have dreamed of asking so personal a question, and of course, our father never volunteered the information."

Marako spoke. "I remember the day he found me crying outside our door. He had heard the other children taunting me because my father was a 'supai.' He took me in his arms and said, 'Remember, Marako, If any man be in Christ he is a new creature. Old things are passed away; behold, all things are become new.'" She gazed out the open window. "He was right, of course. Those words brought me great comfort, but they told me nothing of his innocence or guilt."

"Did someone witness to your father at Manzanar?" Brian asked.

Amy shook her head. "No, my father had heard the message of salvation many times from one who prayed for him years before he accepted the Lord."

"Who?" Addie asked.

A smile touched the faces of all three sisters.

"Oji-san," Amy answered.

CHAPTER 15

Nick's Decision

"If that guy's a Christian, I'm Japanese," Nick declared once they were on their bikes and headed for home.

Brian still had a slightly dazed look on his face, and Addie could hardly believe the news herself. "You know Amy wouldn't say it if it wasn't true, Nick," she said.

"My dad always says God can use anyone," Brian added.

"Why doesn't he try someone with a smile?" Nick was still skeptical.

Addie managed not to giggle. "Come on, Nick. He's very worried right now. Maybe he'd be more . . . personable if Yoshio-san's name was cleared."

"He sure couldn't be any less personable," Nick muttered.

A male pheasant crossed the road in front of them and was soon followed by his mate. Together they disappeared into the thick underbrush by the creek.

"Let's follow them," Brian whispered.

They eased their bikes off the road and laid them quietly in the grass. They tried to slip noiselessly down the bank to the creek below, but the birds heard them and flew away.

"Let's go wading, anyway," Addie suggested. "We haven't been here for weeks."

"Okay," Brian agreed. He left his shoes by Addie's and followed her into the creek. Nick was last off with his sneakers, and soon all three of them were splashing one another and skimming rocks. Addie's throw was much better than it had been at the beginning of the summer and their contest ended with Nick as the winner and Brian and Addie tied for second.

There had been no rain for some time and the creek was shallow. Several large, flat rocks that were normally submerged jutted out of the creek-bed. Addie sat down on one with her feet stretched out in the water in front of her and watched a small plane rise in the sky over Rankin's Air Field.

"I think I would have liked Amy's father," she mused.

"Me, too," Brian agreed. He threw again and his rock skimmed the water gracefully four times before disappearing without a sound. "He must have been a . . ." Brian struggled for the right word. "A strong person," he finally said. "He lived most of his life knowing he was innocent of a crime everyone else believed he committed."

"How do we know he was innocent?" Nick asked

suddenly. Brian and Addie looked at him in surprise. "Well," he said stubbornly, "if he was innocent, why didn't he just come out and *say* he was innocent?"

Addie shrugged. "Saying you're innocent and proving it are two different things."

"Think about it, Nick," Brian said. "How would you prove you're not a spy? I mean, if one government catches you giving information to another government, they can prove you *are* a spy. But how would you prove you're not? How can you be caught... not spying?" His confused look sent Addie into peals of laughter and Nick grinned.

"Don't think about it too hard, Brian," he said. "That would strain even your brain!"

"You know," Addie said when she stopped laughing, "it sounds funny, but maybe Brian's right." She paused and thought hard for several seconds. "Maybe we can still catch Yoshio-san not spying." She sat up straight and her eyes practically glowed with excitement.

"He's dead, Addie," Nick said dryly.

"Quiet." Brian tossed a rock in front of Nick and water splashed up into his face. "What do you mean, Addie?"

"Well, Amy said there might have been an opportunity for her father to be involved in espionage before the bombing of Pearl Harbor. Maybe he was approached by someone in the Japanese government and given secret information, but never passed it on."

"How could we prove that?" Nick was skeptical.

"Find the information," Addie said.

"In the scrapbook," Brian concluded softly.

Addie nodded. "That's where Mr. Yamada thinks it is."

"Addie, we looked all through that book. It was a bunch of drawings. There's no secret information in there," Nick scoffed.

"Then we missed something."

"Maybe you're right, Addie," Brian said, "but even Amy admitted she doesn't know what to look for. How would we?"

"Maybe we should pray about it," Nick muttered.

Brian and Addie exchanged an embarrassed glance. "Not a bad idea," Brian agreed. "Why didn't we think of it?" he asked Addie.

"I was joking," Nick protested. "Don't you think Amy's been praying about this for years? What good has it done her?"

"God doesn't always . . ." Brian began.

"I know, I know," Nick interrupted. "God doesn't always answer our prayers the way we want Him to. Seems to me He doesn't answer them at all, sometimes."

Brian nodded his head in agreement. "Seems that way, doesn't it?" he asked.

It was a quiet reminder of the hardships Brian had been through in the past two years, and Nick was embarrassed.

"Sorry, Brian," he murmured.

"I guess that's what faith is," Brian went on. "Believing that God is in control even when you can't see what He's doing."

"'Now faith is the assurance of things hoped for, the conviction of things not seen,'" Addie said.

Brian nodded. "I got that one quoted at me a lot when Mom was sick."

"What about 'And we know that God causes all things to work together for good to those who love God, . . .'"

"'. . . to those who are called according to His purpose.'" Brian and Addie finished the verse together.

"How can you believe that?" Nick asked bluntly. "Your mom died. What was good about that?"

Brian took a deep breath. "I don't think that verse means her death was a good thing. It means God can cause good things to come from it."

"Like what?"

Brian sat down on a rock next to Addie and Nick joined him. "My mom and dad became Christians about a year before Mom died. I was only eight, but I remember it real well. They weren't getting along, and I would fall asleep at night listening to them argue. I was sure they were going to get divorced."

"Then my mom got cancer. They didn't argue as much, but they still didn't get along very well. Then my dad started going to a Bible Study and pretty soon he became a Christian. When my mom accepted Christ things started to change. Not right away and not all at once, but . . . they changed," he repeated. "I accepted Jesus then, and we started to be a family again. That last year was great."

He bent over and dug several more rocks out of the creekbed. He tossed them, one by one, down the stream and Addie and Nick watched in silence.

Finally he continued. "We prayed and prayed that God would heal my mom. When He didn't, I was mad for a long time. My dad and I talked about it a lot. Dad finally told me I had to choose. I could be angry at God for the rest of my life, or I could believe He knew what was best for Mom. Either way, Mom was in heaven and she *was* healed." He sighed. "I decided to trust God."

He looked at Nick. "That's not really an answer to your question, is it? There's nothing I can point to and say 'This is better because Mom died.' I just know I'm glad she's in heaven, and Dad and I will be with her again someday. What would it be like if we weren't Christians?"

Nick's eyes widened at the thought and he swallowed hard.

"I'm sure Amy feels the same way about her father," Addie said. "She might never prove her father was innocent, but because he was a Christian, she'll always believe God was in control of his life."

"I don't know how anyone can have that much faith," Nick sighed.

"You can't," Brian and Addie both said. Nick looked confused so Brian explained. "No one can generate their own faith. It comes from God. You have to ask Him into your life."

"How?"

Brian grinned. "Now we're back to where we started," he said. "You have to pray."

Nick shook his head. "I wouldn't know what to say."

"When I accepted Jesus, my dad prayed and I repeated his prayer." Brian stopped and took another deep breath. "I could pray with you," he said.

Nick studied his friend for a moment, then nodded, and there in the middle of the creek in the warm September sunshine, he asked Jesus Christ into his life. When they finished praying, Nick looked up to see Addie watching him with eyes suspiciously bright.

"What?" he asked with a shy grin. He gave her a gentle push with his wet toe, but she kept her balance and laughed.

"I was just thinking, Nick. You're going to be the best kind of Christian," she said.

Embarrassed but curious, he asked, "What kind is that?"

"The kind with a smile."

CHAPTER 16

The Scrapbook
is Stolen

Hillary was waiting for them outside their classroom door the next morning before school.

"Did you see the scrapbook?" she asked in an eager whisper.

"Yep." Nick answered her question. "It's full of pictures Nomura drew for Amy and her sisters when they were at the relocation center in Manzanar. It's pretty cool, but I don't think there's anything in it that would prove whether or not he was a spy."

Hillary was surprised by the wealth of information Nick so readily shared. He grinned at her curious expression.

"Class is ready to start," he said. "Let's go, Brian."

"What happened to him?" Hillary whispered to Addie as they followed the boys into the classroom.

"I'll tell you later," Addie whispered back.

Hillary joined them for lunch at noon, and listened quietly to a detailed description of their visit with Amy and her sisters. Addie shared her suspicion that secret information had been hidden somewhere in the scrapbook.

"We need to go back and look at it again. I'm sure we missed something," Addie concluded.

"There's nothing there," Nick insisted.

"If the secret information isn't there, maybe the scrapbook has a clue that tells you where it is hidden," Hillary offered.

"What kind of clue?" Brian asked.

Hillary shook her head. "I don't know. It was just an idea. Maybe Nick's right. Maybe there isn't any secret information anywhere."

"There's something," Addie said firmly. "I'm sure of it. So is Mr. Yamada. Why else would the scrapbook be so important to him?"

"Well," Nick said between bites of his grilled cheese sandwich, "we'll just have to go back and talk to Amy after school today. Maybe she'll remember more about the pictures if she thinks there's a clue hidden in them somewhere."

Hillary sighed. "I wish . . ." she began and hesitated.

"Wish what?" Addie asked.

"Maybe you could come with us, Hillary." It was Nick's suggestion and Hillary stared at him in disbelief.

"You wouldn't care?" she asked.

Nick blushed. "No. I've been kind of . . . a jerk to you lately. I'm sorry."

"That's okay," Hillary answered in a dazed voice. "I'd—I'd like to go if I can find a way out to your house, Addie."

"Maybe you can ride the bus," Addie replied. "I think it's okay with the school if both our moms call the office and make arrangements. Let's go find out."

Together they left the table. On the way to the office, Addie told Hillary about Nick's commitment to the Lord. Hillary was thrilled to hear the good news.

"I knew it had to be *some* kind of miracle," she said with a grin.

The afternoon was hot and it dragged on far too long, but soon all four children were on the bus and headed for home. When they arrived at Addie's, Hillary borrowed Mrs. McCormick's bike and they met the boys in front of Nick's house. They took their time riding to Miss T.'s, first stopping to show Hillary the creek.

"This is so pretty," she exclaimed. "I'd love to live in the country." She watched the other three kick off their shoes. "Can we really go wading?" she cried and was out of her shoes in a flash.

She tromped flatfooted down the stream, soaking herself and anyone within two feet of her. The others laughed at her excitement, but got caught up in the game and soon all four were soaked to the skin and laughing hysterically.

Addie finally waded out and dropped onto the bank, exhausted. Brian followed, then Nick. Hillary came out last and stood dripping over them. She shook her head like a dog and water sprayed in all directions.

"We'll never get dry," she said. "My mom will kill me when she sees my clothes. But it was worth it."

"We'll be dry before you get home," Addie promised. "The air is hot and we're riding bikes. Trust me," she grinned. "We do this all the time."

"You're in for another surprise," Nick said when they were back on the road.

"What's that?" Hillary asked.

Nick pointed ahead to "the mansion" and Hillary gasped. The stately old house looked beautiful in the late afternoon sun. Beds of impatiens bloomed in splashes of color underneath the shady maple trees.

"Is this where Amy lives?" Hillary asked in an awestruck voice.

"With Miss T. Miss T. owns the house," Addie said.

"Miss T. must be rich," Hillary concluded.

"Very well-to-do," Nick grinned. "There she is."

Miss T. was sitting in the rocker on her front porch and she watched the children approach.

"Hi," Addie called.

Miss T. didn't answer, only lifted her hand in acknowledgement. "Something's wrong," Addie said under her breath to the others. "Let's go see what's up."

They left their bikes in the grass and walked up the front steps. Miss T. frowned at the sight of them. "You're soaked," she said to Addie.

"I know," Addie grinned. "We've been wading in the creek. Miss T., this is another friend of ours, Hillary Jackson."

Miss T. nodded. "Nice to meet you, Hillary." A slight pause, then, "You're soaked, too."

Hillary giggled self-consciously. "I know. I'll try not to drip."

"A few drips never hurt anybody," Miss T. said and finally smiled.

"Is Amy home today?" Nick asked.

Miss T.'s smile faded. "She's inside," she said shortly.

Addie heard the familiar click-clack of Amy's funny wooden shoes. The front screen opened and Amy stepped out onto the porch.

"Hello, children," she said softly. When she saw Hillary, her somber face brightened for just a moment. "Hillary! It's nice to see you here. Are you visiting Addie?"

Hillary nodded.

"We wanted to talk to you some more about your scrapbook," Addie said. Amy's face darkened and Addie hurried on before she lost her nerve. "Hillary saw the picture in the paper and started to figure some things out, so we told her about your father and the scrapbook. I hope you don't mind."

Amy shook her head. "Not at all. I know Hillary can be trusted."

Addie glanced at Miss T. and the old woman sniffed loudly. "I can be trusted too, child. I know all about it."

"Good." Addie took a deep breath. "Amy, do you think your father might have had secret information given to him early in the war? Information that he never passed on?"

Amy thought for a moment and then nodded. "I suppose it is possible. Why do you ask?"

"Maybe that's what Mr. Yamada is looking for in your scrapbook."

Amy considered the young girl's eager face. "There is nothing in the scrapbook, Addie," she said sadly. "Only pictures."

"But could there be a clue in the pictures that might tell us where the information is?"

Amy looked hopeful for a brief second, then shook her head. "I do not know."

"Can we look?" Brian asked.

"No." She bowed her head and spoke softly. "The scrapbook is gone."

There was a brief, shocked silence, then Miss T. spoke.

"It's all my fault," she said darkly.

CHAPTER 17

An Unexpected Flight

"What happened?" Addie asked. She sat down on the top step of the porch. Nick leaned against the railing next to Miss T. Brian and Hillary were still the wettest so they stayed off the porch and in the grass.

"Mr. Yamada came back this morning. His grandson came to the door and said they had left an important book here. He asked if he could get it from Amy's room."

Miss T. drummed the arm of her chair with her fingertips. "Amy was in town getting groceries. At that point, I wasn't aware of everything that was going on, and I didn't want to insult her family, so I let him in the house. He was here and gone in less than a minute." She stopped drumming her fingers and smacked the arm of her chair so smartly Brian jumped.

Amy continued the story. "When I returned, Miss Tisdale told me Oji-san had been here. I checked my room immediately, and the scrapbook was gone." Amy rested her hand lightly on Miss T.'s shoulder. "It is my fault. I should have told you the entire story. And I should have locked the scrapbook away. It was careless of me to leave it out."

She sighed. "It is difficult to bear the loss of my father's pictures, but it is almost impossible to believe Oji-san would steal from me."

"Did you see him?" Brian asked suddenly.

"Who? Mr. Yamada?" Miss T. replied.

Brian nodded.

Miss T. frowned and shook her head. "Now that you ask, I don't believe I did. I saw the car in the drive, but I didn't look close enough to see if Mr. Yamada was in it. I just assumed he was."

"And we didn't see him at The Japan House," Brian reminded Addie. "We only saw Kenji in the window. We assumed Mr. Yamada was with him."

He turned to Amy. "I don't believe Mr. Yamada would steal from you either. But would Kenji?"

Amy's eyes clouded over with tears and she closed them briefly. She could only nod in answer to the question and Miss T. patted her arm awkwardly.

"So Kenji has the scrapbook, not Mr. Yamada," Nick concluded. "I'll bet your uncle doesn't even know about this." Nick tried to comfort Amy and she smiled at the young boy's concerned face. "If you call him, maybe he can get the scrapbook back."

"If what you believe is true, I will be greatly relieved," Amy said. "I will call right away, but first I will pray God stops Kenji from any wrong-doing."

Nick nodded vigorously. "Good idea."

His approval was sincere and Addie smiled to herself. Amy heard the change in his voice and studied him curiously.

Nick smiled shyly under her scrutiny and took a deep breath. He spoke so softly Miss T. had to lean forward to hear him. "I'm a Christian now."

"What wonderful news!" Amy exclaimed joyously. "That keeps my problems in the proper perspective. Only eternal things are truly important."

Miss T. was staring wide-eyed at Nick. He shrugged and lifted his hands in self-defense. "What can I say?" he asked with an ornery grin. "Miracles never cease!"

The others laughed, Miss T. loudest of all. "That's an understatement," she declared. But she stood up and ruffled his hair gently. "Good for you," she said. "Good for you."

The ride home was quiet. The late afternoon sun was still hot and a warm breeze dried Hillary off before they reached Nick's house.

When Hillary and Addie got home, they parked their bikes in the garage and went inside. Addie got two fruit drinks out of the fridge and opened a box of crackers.

"Do you think Amy will get her scrapbook back?" Hillary asked Addie.

"She has to." Addie broke two saltines apart with a determined snap. "I know she has a lot of her father's original paintings, but I think that scrapbook is more important to her than any of them. She just has to get it back."

Mrs. McCormick came in from the back yard with a laundry basket full of clean clothes. "Hi, girls." She set the basket on the table and began folding towels. "Who has to get what back?" she asked Addie.

"Do you remember what we told you about Amy and Mr. Yamada, the man in the restaurant?" Addie asked her mother.

Mrs. McCormick nodded.

"Well, there's a lot more to the story now."

"Addie, I thought we told you to stay out of Amy's problems." Mrs. McCormick gave her daughter a stern look.

"It's not that simple, Mom." Addie told her mother all about the picture in the paper and Amy's scrapbook of sketches. "We think that's what Mr. Yamada was after. Only it wasn't Mr. Yamada who wanted it, it was his driver, Kenji. And Dad was right," she added. "Kenji isn't just Mr. Yamada's driver, he's his grandson. And Mr. Yamada is Amy's uncle. But not her father's brother. Her mother's brother."

"What?" Mrs. McCormick was totally confused. Just then Mr. McCormick walked in the back door from work. "Start over," she commanded, "and let your father hear this."

Addie began the entire story again, this time keeping her facts in order. She gave her parents a detailed explanation of the discovery of the sketch from Amy's scrapbook, Mr. Yamada's interest in the scrapbook, his relationship to Amy, and her own belief that secret information was hidden in the scrapbook.

Mr. McCormick sat with his chin in his hand and stared at his daughter. "You can get yourself into the craziest things!" he exclaimed. "I wish I could attribute this to your active imagination, but I'm afraid everything you've said makes sense."

Mrs. McCormick agreed. "It seems to me Amy needs to look through her scrapbook very carefully."

Hillary shook her head. "That's what we were talking about when you came in," she said. "The scrapbook is gone. We think Kenji stole it."

Mrs. McCormick was appalled. "That's terrible! How could anyone even think of stealing from their own relatives?"

"You've heard the expression 'Blood is thicker than water'?" Mr. McCormick asked. "Well, I'm afraid sometimes money is thicker than both of them. The sketches in that scrapbook are probably priceless. He'll be a very rich young man if he can find the right buyer. And that won't be hard."

"I think it's deplorable," Mrs. McCormick said. "If you can't trust . . . oh, dear," she broke off. "Is it 6 o'clock already? There's your mother, Hillary."

Hillary gulped down the last of her fruit drink and took one last cracker. "Thanks for having me out," she told the McCormicks. Addie and her mother walked Hillary out to her car and the two girls talked softly while their mothers chatted.

"I hope your dad's wrong," Hillary said glumly.

"Me too," Addie said. "Amy's got enough bad memories. She deserves to keep her good ones."

The Jacksons left several minutes later and Addie and her mother walked back to the house arm in arm. Inside, her father was on the phone.

"Of course, Eunice. I understand your concern."

Eunice? Eunice Tisdale? Miss T.?

"I can be there in five minutes. No, it's no problem. You're quite welcome. Goodbye."

Her father hung up the phone and his face was grim. "That was Eunice Tisdale."

"What happened?" Addie held her breath, fearing the worst.

"Mr. Yamada arrived at Miss T.'s shortly after you kids left. He was very upset. He went to visit friends this afternoon and when he got back, he found his grandson had packed up and left. Mr. Yamada was sure he would go back for the scrapbook, so the old man drove out to Miss T.'s alone. It took them a while to get him calmed down."

"Then Amy got a call from Sagiri, the woman from The Japan House. It seems she overheard her brother and Kenji talking. They've chartered a private plane out at Rankin's Air Field. They're flying to Chicago and leaving from there to fly to Japan—tonight."

"With Amy's scrapbook!"

"I'm afraid so, honey. I've got to get over there. Mr. Yamada is determined to go to Rankin's and talk to his grandson. Of course, Amy doesn't want to let him go alone. Miss T. suggested perhaps I could go with him. I told her I would."

"Oh, John." Mrs. McCormick was pale. "Do you think it's dangerous?"

He shook his head. "Amy and her uncle both think the boy will listen to reason. But they have to get to him before he leaves."

"Let's go!" Addie was already on her way to the garage.

Her mother followed her out the back door. "Addie, you're not going anywhere."

"Mom!"

"I'm sorry, honey."

"Dad!"

Her father climbed into the driver's seat and Addie ran around the car to the passenger's side. "Please, please, please!"

Mr. McCormick looked at his wife. "Can she stay with Miss T. while I go to the airport?"

Addie started to protest, but her father held up a warning hand. "It's better than nothing, kiddo."

Addie sighed. "All right."

Mrs. McCormick was still frowning, but she nodded. "I hope I don't regret this. Be careful."

Mr. McCormick was already backing out of the garage, but he blew his wife a kiss. Then he and Addie sped down the country road toward Miss T.'s house.

CHAPTER 18

The Scrapbook
Recovered

They reached her corner in record time. Miss T.'s house came into view, but Addie pointed straight ahead. "Look, Dad!"

A dark red car turned the next corner on the mile square, then picked up speed. It was headed in the direction of Rankin's Air Field.

Mr. McCormick slowed down as they approached Miss T.'s house, but there was no sign of Mr. Yamada's car and the front screen door hung open.

He pulled into the drive anyway. "Run up and check, Addie," he said. "Shut the door if they're not here."

Addie ran up the front steps and called out from the doorway. Her voice echoed through the empty house, so she pulled the door closed behind her and shut the screen.

"I was right." She climbed back in the car and fastened her seat belt. "That was Mr. Yamada's car. Let's hurry."

Her father shook his head and muttered to himself, but when he pulled out of the drive he was heading in the direction of the air field. Addie quietly released the breath she had been holding. He was going to let her go along!

They sped down the road once more. Mr. McCormick made a valiant effort to dodge the frequent pot holes, but only succeeded about half the time. After one particularly jarring bounce, Addie looked at the road behind them. "You want to go back, Dad? I think you missed one."

"No smart remarks, young lady," he said gruffly. "You're lucky to be here at all."

When they arrived at the air field, Mr. McCormick drove past the parking lot and directly to the hangar. A small private plane sat on the runway with its engine running. A man with a clipboard stooped to walk underneath the wings, checking his clipboard as he went.

Next to the plane, Mr. Yamada and Amy were deep in conversation with Kenji. Miss T. stood apart from the group, next to the old man's car.

"Stay with Miss T.," Mr. McCormick ordered after parking next to the Nissan. Addie jumped out and ran to the elderly woman.

Miss T. put her arm around the young girl and hugged her close. "I'm so glad you're here. Of course, I can't hear a word they're saying, what with that engine running, but I don't think it's good."

Addie had to agree, judging by the expression on Kenji's face. He looked very angry and was gesturing violently towards the plane. She and Miss T. watched for several minutes as first Kenji, then

Mr. Yamada shouted at one another and waved their arms in the air.

"What's going on?" a voice shouted in Addie's ear and she whipped around in surprise. Nick and Brian stood there on their bikes, sweating and breathing hard.

"Why are you here?" she shouted back.

"We saw your car headed for Miss T.'s so we decided to follow you."

Mr. McCormick looked over and saw Nick and Brian next to Addie. He beckoned to his daughter and she ran to join him.

"Take Miss T. and the boys and wait in the office," he shouted over the roar of the engine. "It's just inside the hangar. Go on," he insisted when Addie began to protest. "There's nothing you can do here."

Addie walked back to her friends and took Miss T.'s arm. "Come on," she yelled. "Dad says we have to wait in the office."

It seemed unusually quiet inside the hangar, although the plane's engine could still be heard. Miss T. shook her head and tapped her hearing aid several times.

"That was just about more than these old ears can handle," she said. She looked around. "Where's the bathroom?" she asked.

"I don't know," Addie replied. There were three more doors in the room and Addie and Brian began opening each one. Nick stayed near the front to watch the scene going on outside. "Here it is," Addie said.

Brian waited until Miss T. had shut and locked the bathroom door, then he gestured frantically to his friends. "Come here, quick!"

Addie and Nick peered cautiously through the door he held open. There was another, smaller room, with a door that opened onto the runway. Through that door they could still see the group by the plane. But Brian wasn't interested in them. Instead, he pointed silently to a small handcart that held two suitcases, a garment bag and a large, black briefcase.

Nick slipped past Brian. He pulled the briefcase off the pile and set it on the floor. Dropping to his knees, he tried to open it, but it was locked.

Addie and Brian exchanged nervous glances. "Nick," Brian began cautiously.

Nick ignored him. "This is one of those combination jobs," he said. "My dad has one like this. Sometimes if you set the tumblers on zero, it will open up." He flipped both sides back to zero and tried again. The case popped open.

Nick lifted the lid cautiously. Inside lay the scrapbook. "All right!" he whispered jubilantly. Addie and Brian were staring at him. "I know. We can't take it. But Amy can. Go get her, Addie."

Before Addie could move they heard a door open in the next room. They all jumped. Nick slammed the briefcase shut and threw it back on top of the luggage. Addie opened the door to the office a crack and peered through. Amy and Mr. Yamada were inside. The frail old man looked tired and beaten and he almost collapsed into one of the white metal chairs that lined the wall.

"Amy!" Addie whispered. Amy looked around her in confusion. Addie opened the door wider. "Over here!"

Amy walked over to them and glanced inside the darkened room. "What are you doing?" she asked in a puzzled voice.

Nick had retrieved the briefcase and opened it once more. He held it up for Amy to see and she gasped in delight. Without hesitation, she reached inside the briefcase and grabbed the scrapbook. Nick shut the case and put it back on the handcart.

The outside door to the runway opened, and the man with the clipboard came in. Kenji was directly behind him, followed by Mr. McCormick.

Amy drew herself up to her full five foot two inches and faced Kenji without flinching. The younger man's black eyes flashed and he began speaking in a torrent of angry Japanese.

When he finally stopped, Amy spoke quietly, in English. "I believe it is in your best interests to follow through with your travel plans. If you remain here, I will call the police."

Kenji started to speak, then thought better of it. He turned and stormed out of the building. The man with the clipboard pushed the handcart out after him, shaking his head and muttering. "Just when I think I've seen it all . . ."

Mr. McCormick took out his handkerchief and wiped his forehead. He looked first at Addie, then Brian, then Nick. They all avoided his gaze and he stuffed his handkerchief back in his pocket. "Where's Mr. Yamada, Amy?" he asked.

She nodded toward the office door. "I must show him the scrapbook," she said and slipped into the next room.

The noise outside increased and Mr. McCormick and the children watched the small plane taxi down the runway and lift smoothly into the air.

"It's all my fault," Nick spoke quickly. Mr. McCormick listened without comment as they watched the tiny plane become a speck in the bright blue sky. "Addie and Brian didn't do a thing. I'm the one who opened the briefcase. They didn't want me to. I knew it was wrong, but I just couldn't let that guy take off with Amy's scrapbook."

Mr. McCormick remained silent.

"I guess I could ground myself," Nick finished lamely.

Mr. McCormick smiled. "Why don't we talk with your parents first?" he asked. He reached over to pull Addie's braid. "Don't look so scared, kiddo. You're not in . . . *too* much trouble."

They filed back into the office. Amy sat next to Mr. Yamada with the scrapbook open on her lap. She smiled warmly at the children and Mr. Yamada acknowledged them with a brief nod.

The bathroom door opened and Miss T. stepped back into the lobby.

"Did I miss something?" she asked.

EPILOGUE

The Court Musician

Kimiko finished pouring the last cup of tea and Marako set a large bowl of rice balls in the middle of the table.

"What are those?" Hillary whispered in Addie's ear.

"Rice balls," she whispered back.

"You'll love them, Hillary," Nick said with a straight face. "Trust me." He helped himself to a rice ball and took a huge bite. "Mmmmm," he said, and Addie and Brian burst out laughing.

"I think I'll pass," Hillary said.

Amy carried two large platters of food into the room and set them on the table. They were both filled with rice and topped with an unusual mixture of chicken and egg.

"This is a very common dish in Japan," Amy said. "It is called *oya-ko donburi*. Oya means parent, ko means child. The chicken and the egg represent that relationship."

Amy took her place at the table and smiled at the group assembled there. Mr. and Mrs. McCormick sat with the children on one side while Amy and her sisters sat on the other. Mr. Yamada and Miss T. were on each end. It had been quite a production helping Miss T. find a comfortable position, but she had insisted on sitting with the others instead of in a chair. "I'm not so old I can't get down on the floor once in a while," she grumbled. "Of course, I might never get up again, but we'll worry about that later."

Now Amy addressed her uncle. "Oji-san, would you bless the food, please?"

Mr. Yamada bowed his head. "Merciful God, your abundant provision for our every need is never-ending. We give you our most heartfelt thanks and pronounce a blessing on this food in the name of Your Son and our Savior, Jesus Christ. Amen."

Amy served Mr. Yamada from one bowl while Marako served Miss T. from the other. Then the dishes were passed down each side of the table and everyone else helped themselves.

"Where's the silverware?" Nick asked, when his search for a fork turned up nothing but a pair of chopsticks.

"We thought you might enjoy eating this meal in the traditional Japanese manner, with *hashi*." Amy demonstrated the proper way to hold the delicate bamboo sticks and ate several bites of chicken in quick succession. The meal went much slower for the children and Addie's parents, but after several false starts they eventually got the hang of chopsticks.

Nick had the most trouble. After three attempts to get a slippery piece of chicken in his grasp, he finally gave up and stabbed it with the end of his hashi.

"That's cheating, Mr. Brady." Miss T. wagged a finger at her young friend and helped herself to another serving of oya-ko donburi. She had surprised everyone with her deft handling of the hashi.

"How'd you learn to do this?" Nick asked.

"My father taught me," she replied. "He could eat spaghetti with his."

The children shouted with laughter at this bit of information. "I'd starve if I had to eat every meal like this," Nick muttered.

"This is delicious, Amy," Mr. McCormick said. He drank the last of his tea and Marako filled his cup again. "It was nice of you to invite us all for dinner after church today."

"I felt there was much we had to celebrate," Amy answered. She smiled at Nick. "Most important of all, we have a new member in our Christian family."

Mr. Yamada spoke next. "We are also most grateful for your help in the past week. I do not know if Yoshio-san's name will ever be cleared of past dishonors." He paused and Amy laid her hand gently on his arm. "But by recovering his book of sketches, you have helped insure that his name will not become the subject of ridicule."

"I read a verse in I Peter this morning that reminded me of your father, Amy," Mr. McCormick said. He pulled a small New Testament out of his shirt pocket. "Here it is. 'For it is commendable if a man bears up under the pain of unjust suffering because he is conscious of God.'"

"Kind of like the emperor's servant," Addie said.

"Is that the emperor in the story?" Nick asked, pointing to the largest doll in the collection on the wall.

Amy smiled. "It could be. I am always reminded of my father's story when I look at the court musician sitting there on the shelf."

The day was warm, but Addie felt goose bumps rising on her arms. "May I look at the court musician?" she asked Amy.

"Of course." Amy was puzzled by the strange request, but she rose to her feet and crossed the room to the stepped shelves. Addie followed her.

Amy took the doll from the shelf and handed it to the young girl. Addie examined it carefully as she turned it first one way and then the other. She ran her finger up and down the doll's back and found what she was looking for. Reaching down the neck of the costume, her fingers touched a piece of paper. She pulled it out slowly.

The paper had been folded in an accordion fashion and was yellow with age. She handed it to Amy without a word. The older woman took it with trembling fingers and opened it. Another paper slipped from its folds, but Amy caught it.

She studied the hidden message for a long time. The room was silent, except for the buzzing of a fly against the window screen.

"What's it say!?" Nick couldn't hold the question back a second longer and everyone in the room let out a collective sigh of relief.

Amy spoke quietly. "It is a note Oji-san wrote my father many years ago." She smiled at her uncle and translated the Japanese characters into English. "'Yoshio-san: For what is a man profited, if he shall gain the whole world, and lose his own soul? Matthew 16:26.' At the bottom, my father has written 'You are right. I cannot do this wicked thing.'" She held out the second piece of paper and Addie gasped when she saw what it was—a $1,000 bill.

"Is that real?" Hillary's voice trembled slightly.

"It might not be accepted as currency today, but I'm sure it was good 50 years ago," said Mr. McCormick.

"Is that all the note says?" Nick asked.

Amy nodded.

"But you'll never know what it is he . . . didn't do."

Amy smiled brightly. "It doesn't matter. It is enough to know he didn't do it."

Amy handed the yellowed piece of paper to Mr. Yamada. The old man's lips moved silently as he read again the words he'd written more than 50 years earlier. Then he clasped the paper gently to his breast, and smiled.

Other Good
Harvest House Reading

KATIE'S WORLD ADVENTURE SERIES

Curious, inquisitive Katie Thompsen loves adventure, loves to travel, and most of all loves to write everything in her diary. So when Katie's journalist father takes the family to faraway places, mystery and misadventure are sure to follow.

You will catch glimpses of the culture and customs of different countries and share Katie's reflections through glimpses into her secret diary. But Katie Thompsen is a special girl because she loves Jesus and loves to learn about the Christian life.

You'll share it all as you discover this exciting new collection of books, the joy of *Katie's World*.

Katie's Swiss Adventure

Katie Sails the Nile

Katie's Russian Holiday

Katie Goes to New York

Katie and the Amazon Mystery

Katie—Lost in the South Seas

The Great Bible Adventure
by *Sandy Silverthorne*

This creative 32-page book is designed with 14 best loved Bible stories set into full double-page illustrations. Every story has several different objects highlighted for the kids to find in the big picture (but watch out—it's gonna be tough!).

The All-Time Awesome Bible Search
by *Sandy Silverthorne*

Hundreds of fun characters crowd into every double-page, full-color illustration. Sprinkled throughout each of the 14 Bible stories are highlighted objects that kids search for in the illustrations. Silverthorne's zany sense of humor drives him to add extra surprises that will have children coming back to see if they've missed anything!

In Search of Righteous Radicals
by *Sandy Silverthorne*

Kids use clues within each of the 14 stories to guess who the main character is. Highlights Bible characters who were radical enough to step out in faith when things seemed impossible—people like Elijah, Nehemiah, Peter, and Ruth. A one-sentence wrap-up woven into each story reinforces the important lesson kids learn from their Bible heroes.